G000143764

The Streets of Laredo

by the same author

The Last Romantic Out of Belfast

The STREETS of LAREDO

Sam Keery

To John Glen
with best wishes
S Keery

JONATHAN CAPE
THIRTY-TWO BEDFORD SQUARE LONDON

First published 1986

Jonathan Cape Ltd, 32 Bedford Square, London WC1B 3EL

British Library Cataloguing in Publication Data

Keery, Sam
The streets of Laredo.
I. Title
823'.914[F] PR6061.E4/

ISBN 0-224-02373-X

The author and publishers are grateful to Faber and Faber Ltd for permission to reproduce three lines from 'The Love Song of J. Alfred Prufrock' from *Collected Poems 1909–1962* by T. S. Eliot, which appear on p. 112.
'A Grounding in the Classics' previously appeared in the *Belfast Review* and 'Lily of Laguna' was first published in the *Fiction Magazine*.

Printed in Great Britain by
Ebenezer Baylis & Son Ltd
The Trinity Press, Worcester and London

To Sheri

Contents

The Floating Off of Mr Triggs

Mr Triggs was a bit of a card. It wasn't that he had set out to be a card or had to work at it like other cards: for example, the Assistant Comptroller, who was seen in the corridors with his glasses pushed up on his forehead, and when junior staff bid him good morning would reply – 'Oh, er, good morning to you, er, whoever you are', in order that they would go about saying what a *card* he was. Mr Triggs was not like that.

Mr Triggs sometimes let out a loud fart at his desk, to the amusement of some of the male, but not the female, clerks. One woman became incensed when Mr Triggs farted, though she was unable to refer to it directly and merely banged filing cabinet drawers and gave black looks in Mr Triggs's direction. But then she was famous for holding strong views on women's rights and one of the department wags said that it was not so much Mr Triggs's farting that annoyed her as that it was something only *men* could get away with.

When Mr Triggs farted he sometimes went on working with his head down, so that it would not have been obvious it was him except that nobody else ever did it; at other times he sat up startled, and then looked carefully under his desk and peered into drawers, this being his *little joke*.

Mr Triggs was very thin, with a vaguely ecclesiastical air like a bumbling curate. He had large feet on the end of spindly legs and was easy to spot at a distance. He was often seen standing among the middle-aged men watching the girls play basketball in Lincoln's Inn. He would be at the goal where there was most activity in order to get a good view of the girls' knickers as they leapt up at the basket or rushed stooping to pick up the ball. There were two courts and Mr Triggs would move from one to the other depending on which game was showing the most knickers.

Mr Triggs said that when he retired he was going to go up to the management corridor and do an 'up yours' sign at every one of the doors. He was inclined to say this at lunchtime drinks when he drank brown stout and spoke of his wartime experiences in the Army Catering Corps. Somebody suggested he should fart as well, at which Mr Triggs merely smiled inscrutably. He never acknowledged his farting.

Mr Triggs's main interest in life was his model steam railway engine. He was an authority on model engines. He never referred to his model as a model but as his Pacific Class 4-6-2 which he was in the process of constructing. It had been in this state for many years and was not therefore actually working, but it would one day. Every year when he was passed over for promotion he spoke of asking for an early pension so that he could work on his Pacific Class 4-6-2.

Some afternoons he would doze off at his desk, sitting upright with his head nodding on to his chest. The younger clerks would throw balls of paper at him for a lark or make a sudden terrible noise to wake him. Being caught dozing embarrassed him and made him angry in a way that being caught farting should have done but didn't. When this happened he started slamming drawers and being very short with people.

Occasionally he came into possession of a girlie magazine. He would look through it at his desk with the same seriousness with which he would study his railway books and magazines before carefully putting it away. Clerks near his desk would be startled by the sight of Mr Triggs gazing somewhat coldly at the large centre-spread picture of a naked girl with bushy pubic hair. He would take it home, he said, and study it there. Home? Mr Triggs was as much married as any of them. What if the wife caught him? He would look at it in his den, he said. His den was where he worked on his

Pacific Class 4-6-2 and where his wife never ventured. Some of the men said, 'Oh-ho, so that's what you have your toy trains for.' But this was not true. Mr Triggs's interest in trains could be seen to be genuine from the way in which he denounced what he called the cock-ups on the suburban rail services that made people late at the office. Mr Triggs always saw through the bland excuses that were put out by British Rail because he knew all about up-working and down-working and loop lines and single track signalling. Mr Triggs was the Secretary of his local model steam railway club and his pet subject was how stick-in-the-mud they were. One of his battles was to get them to admit traction engine people – he just needed two more votes at the Annual Gen., he said. This had been the position for some years, and the morning after the railway club Annual Gen. found Mr Triggs in almost as bad a temper as the morning after the annual promotion list was put up when Mr Triggs had to face the wife with the news that he had been passed over yet again, notwithstanding his being a distant relative of other Triggses who had been in much more senior positions in the firm.

An uncle of Mr Triggs had once risen to be a Comptroller. Mr Hoddle, the Deputy Chief Clerk on the department, remembered him well because Mr Hoddle was an office boy at the time and had to light the fire in Mr Triggs's office every morning. And woe betide you if it went out! Any reference to bygone days in the firm, such as Mr Hoddle having to carry in coals and poke the previous Mr Triggs's fire, always evoked from the older clerks recollections of high-top desks with stools; of famous cards (if their names were Miller they were always 'Dusty' Miller, if Clark 'Nobby' Clark and so on); of the strict segregation of women and the absurd lengths to which this was taken, such as separate times for morning tea in the basement canteen. The female clerk who had made a name for herself as a women's rights fanatic tended to bring these reminiscences to an end by banging drawers and saying loudly that it hadn't changed at all, only on the surface, that women were as discriminated against as ever.

The present Mr Triggs said that they had had a maid when

he was a child in the south London suburb of Streatham. He said that kind of thing over his bottle of brown stout at lunchtime drinks. When his uncle the Comptroller was a Chief Clerk he had been served sherry for his elevenses, not tea. 'Sherry! Get away,' said the younger element, quite used to the Chief Clerk coming away from the vending machine with a plastic cup just like the rest of them. '*Sic transit gloria mundi*,' said Mr Hoddle, who rumour had it had been to boarding school, as his accent was a bit more middle class than you would expect in a Deputy Chief Clerk who would go no further.

There were lunchtime drinks for all kinds of reasons: promotions; birthdays; births; marriages; transfers to or from other departments. These last were called 'floating on' or 'floating off' drinks. When Mr Hoddle 'floated himself on' from a department that was being computerised, he was seen to be a bit of a card, judging from his accounts of the rows he had with motorists when riding his bicycle from Whitechapel – if a car came too close he spat on the windscreen just where the wiper could not reach. It was at Mr Hoddle's 'floating on' drink that Mr Triggs claimed he had once heard his uncle the Comptroller saying that when he retired he was going to go up on to Management corridor and do an 'up yours' sign at every one of the doors. 'Get away,' they said, 'a Comptroller!' Even Mr Hoddle could not take that in, having once had to look after his coal fire and run messages, but Mr Triggs assured them it was so. Mr Triggs then acted out the way his uncle the Comptroller had said he was going to do the 'up yours' sign: he put his brown stout down on the bar and took a few steps as if coming to the carpeted and panelled hush of Management corridor; then he swung his arm up in a huge arc from the floor with two fingers in a V high above his head and blowing a long loud raspberry with his tongue that made people all along the bar stare in surprise.

'He never did it,' said Mr Triggs regretfully, and people noted that Mr Triggs had referred to his uncle *once* saying that at a family wedding. Perhaps it was just that the occasion had been too much for him. It was impossible to conceive of a

Comptroller doing *that* on Management corridor! All the staff went there once a year for their annual interviews and the oak panelling and thick piled carpet made them very subdued as they waited in groups for their names to be called. Some of the younger ones would be sent home by their Heads of Department to put on a white shirt. They would be called a long time before the Manager saw them, in order not to waste his time. Mr Hoddle's 'floating on' drink, at which Mr Triggs told the story of the 'up yours' sign, was just after the annual interviews.

Both Mr Triggs and the women's rights fanatic had taken their being passed over rather badly. She had actually made a slight scene on Management corridor, to the embarrassment of the groups being marshalled by the secretaries. She had come out of a Manager's office looking very flushed and angry. 'This firm does nothing for women,' she said very loudly, as she walked past the groups who were in a state of subdued excitement over who had got a promotion and who had got an increment.

It was a point of honour for most, though not all, of those who had been expecting a promotion but had not received one to be the first to congratulate those who had. Mr Triggs was not one of these. He tended to sulk and to have to be rallied in a long session with the Chief Clerk, who tried his best to assure him that it wasn't because his face didn't fit. Mr Triggs suggested bitterly that it was more to do with the fact that he spoke his mind rather than being somebody's blue-eyed crawler and the Chief Clerk admitted with a sigh that there might be something in that. The sigh was meant to indicate that he might have got further himself but for similar independence of spirit. This part of their little heart-to-heart, conducted in the Chief Clerk's box which was only head high and had no doors, was overheard by some of the younger men who thought it hilarious, since both Mr Triggs and the Chief Clerk addressed all superiors as 'sir'. It quite irritated the younger clerks, indeed it got on their wicks, to listen to Mr Triggs bowing and scraping on the telephone, 'sirring' left, right and centre. One of them would make a mark on his pad every time Mr Triggs said 'sir' during a telephone conversation, and then would count the marks, loudly announcing the score – which everybody but Mr Triggs knew the meaning of. In all fairness to Mr Triggs, these conversations sometimes took the following form. 'Well, sir, with respect, sir, I hope you don't mind me saying so, sir, but that's a load of rubbish, sir.'

Moreover it was just after such a telephone conversation that Mr Triggs would be most likely to let off one of his famous farts.

There came rather an eventful year. The computer was installed. There were many 'floating on' and 'floating off' drinks. Mr Triggs finally defeated the conservative anti-traction engine diehards at the railway club Annual Gen. Mr Hoddle was pursued into the office by a taxi driver who, as they said, 'laid one on him' at the war memorial in the courtyard. The woman who spoke so bitterly about its being a man's world was retired prematurely on a reduced pension and was soon remembered only for the little protest she had made on Management corridor – though her kind of eccentricity would not be recollected to evoke nostalgia for time past, as with the oddities and foibles of the 'Dusty' Millers and 'Nobby' Clarks. Then Mr Triggs was taken seriously ill.

His illness came as a surprise to his colleagues. He had seemed so wiry and tough, striding about in his narrow trousers worn high up to reveal his spindly ankles. They said jokingly he hardly had to roll them up when he paddled in the sea on his holidays. The younger clerks had a good laugh making up images of Mr Triggs on old-fashioned seaside holidays: sunbathing in vest and braces, his head covered with a handkerchief knotted at the four corners. Mr Triggs had not minded these jokes in the least; he had even encouraged them by sending old-fashioned postcards of the fat women/red-nosed men sort when he went away, even though his holidays were of the kind that catered for railway enthusiasts – such as a week on a Welsh narrow gauge quarry railway. He was taken ill right in the middle of organising a week on a Portuguese narrow gauge quarry railway.

He was gone a long time. They sent him a signed-by-everybody funny 'get-well' card with a bed-pan joke on it, overruling Mr Hoddle, who had wanted to send a fat-woman postcard which they considered would have been in bad taste. There was talk of lighter duties when he returned – possibly on another department – which would mean a 'floating off' drink. Mr Hoddle had to go through Mr Triggs's drawers. Some of the men expected him to turn up naughty magazines but they were disappointed in the various publications that came to light: *A History of the London-Brighton and South-Coast Railway*; *Know Your Blowlamp (3) – Advanced*; *The Oil-Fired Loco, Is It Cheating? – The Case For Coal.* However Mr Hoddle did occasionally emit little cries of, 'Streuth! He's still got one of these,' or, 'Gawd, this takes you back a bit,' as he held up objects that had been standard office issue years before. The Chief Clerk called out to him with mock severity that he wasn't to make it a trip down memory lane, but even he joined in playing with the small brass and iron calculating machine and showed the younger clerks how to set up the figures and get the answer by twirling the little crank handle at the end. Mr Hoddle had only just finished clearing the contents of the desk into a tea chest when the news came that Mr Triggs was dead.

A large party from the firm went to his funeral. At first this was to be quite unofficial, but then the Comptroller in charge of the group of departments thought that the firm should do something for such a long-serving employee. The term 'old servant' was used, though it was not clear by whom. The younger element turned this phrase over in wonder and repeated it, fascinated. *Old servant.* It belonged so much to the days of stools, high-topped desks and wing-collared Chief Clerks who looked like Neville Chamberlain that it was incredible that it should have survived into what everybody was calling the 'Computer Age'.

The Comptroller sent round a memorandum in which the box headed 'Subject Matter' contained the words: 'Funeral of Mr Triggs'. It invited those wishing to attend the funeral of the above in addition to what it designated the Official Party to submit their names to Personnel. The Official Party, which included the Comptroller himself, would take the Official Wreath, which, it emphasised, should be the only one from the firm (this was to discourage people having a 'whip-round' for a wreath: there had been several instances when the 'whip-round' wreath was much bigger than the Official one). The memorandum set out how much time off would be granted, making it clear that only the Official Party would be able to claim travelling expenses. There would be a taxi to transport the Official Party from the station to the crematorium and if others wished to hire additional taxis at their own expense would they please let Personnel know as soon as possible.

Mr Hoddle took umbrage at not being in the Official Party, particularly as Mr Paget was – despite his being only a Section Leader. This was because Mr Paget had been the one to take the call from Mr Triggs's wife about his death and informed the Comptroller before telling the Chief Clerk. He had conveyed the sad news very impressively with just the proper tone of regret and solemnity. Passed away in the night. Mr Paget also took it upon himself to organise the names of those who wanted to go at their own expense, though if they asked about the arrangements in such a way as to suggest that they thought that Mr Paget would be going with *them* he would point out that *he* was one of the Official Party in the same unctuous tones that he had used for phrases like 'passed away in the night'.

Mr Hoddle was in charge of the 'whip-round' to pay for the taxis for people not in the Official Party. Mr Hoddle was very good at organising 'whip-rounds' for all sorts of things, many of them to do with drinking, and had assumed that he would be allowed to organise the funeral party on a 'whip-round' basis. He was very annoyed at the way Mr Paget stepped into the Official Party taxi at the station and stood about with the Official Party at the crematorium.

The crematorium was running late. It was two funerals behind schedule. When Mr Triggs's funeral was due to start the card on the door of the chapel saying which service was going on inside still had a time on it of an hour previously. The hearse of the next funeral was waiting in the long tree-lined driveway while the minister kept looking out of the changing room to see if it was his turn yet. A row of wreaths had been laid out on the beautifully kept lawn and people walked round them reading the cards. These wreaths belonged to the funeral previous to the one going on in the chapel. At one end of the chapel was a chimney to which the younger clerks in the Unofficial Party raised their eyes surreptitiously from time to time in sly guilty excitement. A girl official in a kind of cassock waited to remove these wreaths and replace them with those belonging to the funeral taking place in the chapel so that the people attending it could look at the wreaths and read the cards in their turn. Several other parties were therefore hanging about as well as the firm's Official Party and the Unofficial Party. They passed the time strolling in the beautiful grounds or reading the plaques on the brick wall specially built for the purpose. Some of the plaques only had names and dates; others said things like 'His soul liveth for evermore' or 'Darling Bunty'.

Mr Hoddle's Unofficial Party stopped to watch two robins squaring up to each other in the middle of a shady path. The robins were reluctant to give way to the strolling group, which was amused when Mr Hoddle eagerly pointed out how the little birds resumed their dispute after the party had passed. Mr Hoddle said that robins were the most territorial birds in the world. Spent all their time seeing other robins off their property. 'Even interfered with their courtship,' said Mr Hoddle authoritatively. People looked at each other in surprise but, before they could ask him how he knew all that and make jokes about the only *birds* they thought he watched, they saw another hearse enter the gate and come to a halt in the drive and the word passed round that it was Mr Triggs.

When Mr Triggs's hearse slid swiftly forward to the door of the chapel a young Anglican priest hurried out of the changing room. Mr Triggs's coffin was carried into the chapel and all the parties followed solemnly behind. At last the clerks saw the widow and relatives. So that was Mrs Triggs. After all those years during which she had been known to them only by Mr Triggs's references to Gladys. Gladys says this; Gladys won't eat that. She was as nondescript in appearance as Mr Triggs. A separate party sat in pews at the back and the whisper went round that they were from the railway club. The younger clerks who had never before been to a cremation kept stealing glances at the little black curtain on the wall, towards which the coffin was pointed on a rollered chute. The young minister said 'our dear friend Edward' at the appropriate point in the service. Not Edward Triggs. Just Edward. Was that traditional or the new way of doing things? Like some of the words they sang to a well-known psalm which were different from the words they were used to? The order of service was printed in a little booklet and people listened with surprise to each other saying the responses. Mr Hoddle in particular astonished people by the firm way he spoke the responses without looking at the booklet, and the way he sang very loudly the 23rd Psalm with slightly different words from those printed – for it was widely believed that Mr Hoddle's only pastime was drinking. The Comptroller did not merely crouch over the pew rack like the others but slipped on to his knees on the cushions provided and held his hand across his brow in a manner that was very impressive.

Although there was no evidence of the presence of crematorium staff, there came a moment when the younger clerks noticed with a thrill that the black curtain was slowly parting and the coffin began to slide gently forward. Did the minister push a bell, they wondered, or did the people behind the scenes know from the prayers? But they would be different for all the different sects and religions. Naturally none of them voiced these questions, and in few seconds Mr Triggs slid into whatever lay behind that black curtain and suddenly all his life was over: his childhood in a house that had a maid; his war record in the Catering Corps; the unfinished Pacific Class 4-6-2 in his den; his failure to do an 'up yours' sign on Management corridor. It was impressive, even awesome, and yet it would fade more quickly than the already fading image of the tea chest beside the empty desk.

Mrs Triggs shook hands with the Official Party and invited them back to the house. Mr Paget stepped into the Official Party car with the same gravity of manner that had impressed the Comptroller. Mr Hoddle suggested a 'whip-round' for a drink among the older clerks before returning. The younger ones went back enlivened by an interesting experience but frustrated by propriety from eagerly discussing it.

Mr Hoddle's 'whip-round' drink lasted till closing time and was joined by the Chief Clerk. When they eventually returned to the office the Chief Clerk and Mr Hoddle continued noisily to recall old times in the Chief Clerk's box. Even when they lowered their voices to what they thought were confidential tones they still boomed out over the top of the box or through the doorless side panel. Don't make them like Eddie Triggs any more. This younger generation. Can't tell them apart sometimes. Not like old Eddie. Used to be all a bit like that. Half the clerks in London used to go a bit funny like old Eddie. Not the same now. No *flavour* to them!

The young Assistant Comptroller hove into view, but hesitated. He had been intending to convey his displeasure at so many of the department's phones being left unattended but thought better of it when he saw the state in which that man Hoddle had brought back the Chief Clerk from the Triggs funeral. As if an up-ended bicycle with the tube hanging out in a Visitor's Interview Room wasn't enough for one week! And if you mentioned it over lunch the old fogies said, 'Oh well, you know, a long-serving man, an old servant.' The Assistant Comptroller decided to duck quickly back into his office, but he was not quick enough for Mr Hoddle who thought it his duty to tell the Chief Clerk that *sir* seemed to want him.

'Look at *sir*,' he shouted at the Chief Clerk, pointing with outstretched arm at the young Assistant Comptroller as if he was a dim speck on the horizon, 'sir wants you. Don't you, sir. Don't go away, sir. He's right here, sir.'

The Chief Clerk rose to his feet a little unsteadily – even though he had given Mr Hoddle what he thought was a safe head-start before joining the drinks in the pub. His spectacles were just ever so slightly askew.

'We were giving Eddie Triggs a good send-off, sir,' he shouted sadly.

'Floating off old Eddie Triggs, sir,' Mr Hoddle confirmed, 'we were just floating off old Eddie.'

Heritage

It was such a warm day that a porter was called to open slightly the large stained-glass windows of the conference hall of the Bulwark Assurance Company. Some of the men who were assembled in rows below the platform muttered to each other that it would have been better to allow them to take off their jackets rather than let in the noise of the market on the street below. But although, as the Chairman said in his address, they lived in a time of great social change, none of the district managers gazing up at the platform was going to be the first to rebel against ties and jackets on a hot autumn day, though they knew perfectly well that the days of traditional office protocol were numbered. There was even a shocked whisper going round the district offices that the staff associations at Chief Office, even the ladies' section, had been holding hush-hush meetings with a *trade union*! The Chairman did not refer to this directly, but spoke with great feeling about heritage, values, standards, traditions, the weathering of storms. He made it clear that when he spoke of these things he meant them to apply not only within the company. This great company of theirs was itself a national institution; 'the man from the Bul' had become a household phrase, part of the very warp and woof of the rich tapestry of the nation's life, of the nation's heritage. With steady hands at the helm they had weathered storms triumphantly in the past and he had no doubt that they would together, standing shoulder to shoulder, weather once more the storms for which the clouds were now gathering. The Chairman spoke feelingly of how uplifted and inspired he had been on his recent tour of the district offices. He would say here what he had said to the board: *our men are in good heart*, he had said, *we must not let them down*. He made no apology for reminding them yet again of the time when the shadow of nationalisation by a socialist government had hung over them, of how humble employees had come up to him with tears in their eyes, asking if nothing could be done, of how they had all seemed to be supinely awaiting their fate, of how, one day, during a gloomy game of golf with the Chairman of the Rampart, he had suddenly turned to him and said, 'Why *should* we?' The Chairman implied that this now celebrated golf course utterance, made before teeing off at the eighteenth, had roused them all to stand fast and fight. He was heartened by the new business premiums being collected in the length and breadth of the land by *men in good heart* whose swords would not sleep in their hands to resist the wreckers.

Murmurs of sympathetic indignation came from the audience. Even the younger ones, the top-selling salesmen brought over for a hand-shake from the General Manager and who sweated resentfully in their office suits, were deeply impressed. They sat up in their seats and stopped exchanging amused looks with each other at some of the sounds from the market which occasionally drifted up to punctuate the pauses in the Chairman's speech.

'I'm not asking five pounds; I'm not asking four pounds; never mind three pounds; 'ere, I tell you what I'll do . . . '

'Knickers,' a deep male voice announced gravely, 'free fittings behind the stall.'

'Nine-carat gold, five shillings, how does he do it they ask?'

'Knickers. As worn by Royalty.'

'Eighteen-carat gold, seven shillings and sixpence.'

'Knickers. Guaranteed identical to those worn by Princess Margaret.'

Not the least impressive feature of the Chairman's peroration was his complete indifference to the noises-off. 'Never batted an eyelid,' they said afterwards admiringly, 'nothing ever ruffles him, won the DFC in the Battle of Britain.'

In good heart. Tradition. Our national heritage. None was more affected by these sentiments than Sammy Mercer, one of the Belfast men. Whereas the others in the Belfast contingent would have preferred to take more advantage of being in London without the wife to keep an eye on them, Sammy would have been happy looking at places like the Tower, Downing Street, St Paul's Cathedral. Nor could they just let him go his way and they theirs. It was not as simple as that. Sammy was the oldest of them, and, although an affable gregarious man fond of a drink or two, he was also very old-fashioned, church-going, disapproving of blue jokes, courteous to women – raised his hat to them, opened doors for them, all that sort of thing. He was therefore held in high regard by the wives of the London party, whose task of slowly extracting from their husbands what they had got up to in London by means of seemingly casual questioning was made simpler because of Sammy's presence in the team. The debriefing tended to concentrate on whether Sammy had been with them on each of their evenings *all the time*.

Sammy sang in his church choir and had a rich deep voice. People said he should have been a preacher or a politician, so fond was he of quoting famous sayings, biblical texts, lines of verse, memorable phrases. 'The glory that was Greece, the grandeur that was Rome.' 'Never give a sucker an even break.' 'Cannon to right of them, cannon to left of them . . . ' 'Get the name of early riser and you can sleep till noon.' 'Youth a folly, manhood a struggle, old age a regret.' In the public house after the Chairman's speech the mood was one of nostalgia for the time of past greatness and they spoke of the tragedy of the Belfast-built *Titanic*, and of the biggest Unionist gathering of all time when 100,000 people had sung 'Oh, God, Our Help in Ages Past'. Mention of this famous hymn gave Sammy the opportunity to hold forth on one of his favourite themes: The World's Great Hymns. By this he meant the hymns sung on public occasions: football matches; round gravesides; at political demonstrations; on the decks of sinking ships, hymns like 'Abide with Me' or 'Lead Kindly Light'. They were, Sammy pronounced with a confident gravity which showed that he had had practice in saying it, hymns that *did not offend the unbeliever*, hymns that anybody could sing: Protestants, Catholics, Hottentots.

'Change and decay in all around I see,' said Sammy sonorously, rolling out the words with his chin lowered to his chest to give added resonance, 'lovely words. Lovely words.'

He personally thought that 'Lead Kindly Light' was the finer. The *finer*, mark you, not necessarily the better. He made the distinction between fine and coarse. It didn't pay to be too fine in this world, he advised them gloomily, or you'd get yourself walked on and didn't he bloody know it. It was the same everywhere in the world you're in today, be a bit nice to people and they'll wipe their bloody feet on you, be a bit better than them at something and they'll try to pull you down. Insurance. The Church. Friends and neighbours were just as bad, maybe the worst of the lot, jealousy and envy ruling the roost, as he was never done telling that son of his, lying in an armchair reading books, waiting for people to take him by the hand.

'Lead kindly light, amid the encircling gloom,' recited Sammy reflectively, 'ah, great words, great words. Of course that's a great Catholic hymn.'

'A Catholic hymn?' they queried in surprise, one of them, a keen Orangeman, in consternation.

'Oh pardon me,' Sammy assured them with authority. He did a piece of mime involving leafing through *Hymns Ancient and Modern*, traced his finger down an imaginary page till it stopped at 'Lead Kindly Light' and read out sternly the name of the composer. John Henry Newman. *Cardinal* Newman.

St Paul's Cathedral was near, and to humour Sammy they strolled into it before setting out for their evening's drinking. With neckties off and open shirts they enjoyed the coolness coming from the marble that was everywhere shaded by the echoing spacious chambers, crypts, private chapels, even though these teemed with tourists from many countries. Some were herded by guides who harangued their parties in their native languages, revealing the names of men and places that had significance in British history. Wellington. Christopher Wren. Trafalgar. John Donne. The Blitz. Men in ecclesiastical vestments sold tickets at turnstiles, and now and then flashbulbs of cameras lit up some artefact with a lurid light.

It so happened that it was one of the days during which the cathedral was being used to stage a piece of scientific history. An experiment was being carried out, which, a notice said, had last been done in the eighteenth century. An area directly under the great dome had been cordoned off to allow the movement to and fro of a bronze globe swinging on a thick cable stretching so far upwards, that, to the people craning their necks below, it seemed to dwindle first to a delicate thread and then to become invisible long before they could trace it to its anchor somewhere under the great gilded bowl. With each mighty swing of the sphere a little spike on the bottom cut a new mark on a ridge of sand, showing that the pendulum did not quite return to where it started from because the earth's rotation in the interval would not allow its motion to be a perfect arc but wobbled it from the true so faintly that it needed a cathedral to measure precisely the extent of the corruption. The Belfast men watched, wonderstruck, as the golden ball glided to and fro silently, beautifully, in a seemingly perfect purity of motion, had it not been for the tell-tale marks on the sand as the world shifted ceaselessly under their very feet. It might have been the subject of a sermon by the great John Donne from the pulpit of St Paul's on the tiny quantum of irreversible change within each passing moment, on the impossibility of ever going back to what had been the moment before.

'They're open,' one of them said to break the reflective silence, meaning the public houses.

'Nelson's tomb,' said Sammy, as if striking a bargain, 'while we're here and still sober.'

Others too were gazing at the magnificent mausoleum of the hero of Trafalgar, including a group of French schoolchildren who were being lectured by their teacher in their own language in an attempt, probably vain, to explain the importance to the British of what in the children's history books would have been glossed over as an indecisive naval engagement off Ushant in the time of their revered Napoleon. An American woman told her companion that this one must be the guy that sank the Armada after a cricket match. One of Sammy's companions asked them if they minded the Halloween game about Nelson's eye they'd played when they were children, the one where you were led in blindfolded and made to feel somebody lying down. This is Nelson's foot. This is Nelson's leg. This is Nelson's arm – it was an empty sleeve. This is Nelson's . . . and they poked your finger into something mushy like a rotten apple! Knew a fella that threw up once, isn't the power of suggestion marvellous?

'England this day expects,' Sammy recited musingly, turning over the famous words from his rag-bag collection like a magpie with its store of bright beads.

From the steps of the cathedral they could see the sign of a public house. Someone wondered if that was the one with the dirty pictures on the wall. No, he was told, that was the Cheshire Cheese further down. Fleet Street. Not pictures. Tiles. Very naughty tiles. To do with Samuel Johnson it seemed. He spent a lot of his time there. These tiles. All the positions. Sammy here would know about Samuel Johnson. 'When a man, sir, is tired of London, he is tired of life,' said Sammy. Somebody remarked that this fella in costume took parties to see the tiles. Expected a tip. A woman on a man's lap being hoisted up and down on pulleys, he keeps to the last. Tst tst. Disgusting. Not worth it. Did you hear that fella in the market hawking the knickers! Chairman took it real cool. As cool as bloody Barnum. Who?

'The greatest showman of all time,' explained Sammy admiringly, 'sure you must have heard of Barnum. *If you don't advertise your goods, the sheriff will advertise them for you*. Phineas Barnum. Showed Buffalo Bill and Tom Thumb to the crown heads of Europe. Was ruined once. Never turned a hair. Asleep when the news came.' Sammy made believe to hold before him a piece of paper bearing the awful message. 'The landlady at the bedside,' intoned Sammy gravely, 'with the telegram. *Barnum's burnt to the ground.* And Barnum turned on his side and went to sleep again!'

Knickers. Tired of London, tired of life. Woman on a man's lap. What about the West End for a good booze-up? Couldn't go home without seeing the town. And perhaps . . . But they left the *perhaps* thoughts unspoken. Each had his own idea about how far *perhaps* might go. Stare at the whores on a Soho pub crawl. See a blue movie. As to . . . *want a short time, dearie?* . . . The obstacle was not just Sammy. Even if they got Sammy tanked up blind they dared not trust each other. They belonged to that class of men whose sexual uncertainty when young had expressed itself not so much in bashfulness and timidity but in grabbing hastily for a partner soon after puberty, 'going steady' from about seventeen, engagement at eighteen with full sexual relations twice weekly, early marriage, children, early middle age, and they were chronic sufferers from dissatisfaction at having missed out on excitements and joys.

Sammy fell behind to light his pipe, a habit of his which was a perennial bone of contention between him and his wife. She often found herself alone suddenly when she thought he was alongside her on a street and he would be a hundred yards back striking matches for that blessed pipe of his. Now, when the insurance men looked round for him, he was nowhere to be seen. They asked each other in consternation where he could be. Was the Old Bailey near there? Could Sammy have turned off to gape at it – he was a sucker for places like that?

But even as they debated the alarming mystery Sammy suddenly reappeared, stepping out of the public convenience they had passed without noticing, puffing at his pipe, still belatedly doing up his fly. He had just stepped in to make his water, he explained, and got talking to this Englishman alongside him. He had told him he had just come from St Paul's but wished it had been a Sunday for he'd love to go to a service there. The man had told Sammy he'd never been to a service in his life. Do you worship nowhere on a Sunday then, Sammy had asked him, saying that where he came from everybody went someplace, be it only a tin-roofed gospel hut.

'Oi don't believe in it meself,' Sammy mimicked thoughtfully in a bad imitation of a London accent, and said that he had told the man that he wondered about these things himself and thought sometimes that he only went for the singing.

Sammy, Sammy, they scolded him, what did the English people care whether he went to church or not. What a place to be debating religion in! But it was clear that Sammy would long muse on his encounter with the unbeliever in the gents'. Maybe he would work it into his discourse on the World's Great Hymns, the hymns that anybody could sing on public occasions. 'The night is dark and I am far from home, Lead thou me on.' Sure that fella could sing it along with the rest, Sammy would say, that fella alongside him in the public convenience.

At the bottom of Ludgate Hill Sammy fell behind again, but this time they kept an eye on him as he stopped to light his pipe and gaze back up the hill at St Paul's, silhouetted against the evening sky, the golden cross upon its dome shining out over the great pagan city in the setting sun. Sammy stood marvelling at the beauty and majesty of the great monument to belief. He marvelled too at the unbelief, so casually uttered, so lightly carried, which he had encountered in its very shadow.

'Knickers as worn by Royalty,' somebody said with a laugh, and another asked if they were all in good heart to join the union.

Our Ivy

Ivy Litvinoff Returns to the Office was the title of the piece in the company magazine. It was not a large piece and could easily have been passed over by cursory readers whose attention would have been more readily attracted by the latest batch of promotions and retirements; the scores in sports leagues for football, cricket, rifle shooting; thrilling first-hand accounts of package tours to the Pyramids or Disneyland; reviews of stage productions by the Drama Society with pictures of our familiar colleagues less familiar in costume and make-up (Lucy Major's Lady Bracknell . . . the performance we have come to expect over many years); and a lengthy nostalgic description by a pensioner of how-it-used-to-be-in-the-dear-old-office. What a jolly prank the 1926 General Strike had been for the girls in the make-shift dormitory on the fifth floor . . . larking about after lights-out throwing things at each other . . . pair of knickers flew out of the window and – oh dear! – landed on the sill of the Chief Actuary whose office was – oh heavens! – locked for the night . . .

Ivy Litvinoff too had lived through stirring events but was more discreet. She had been a typist before the First World War. Used to work on the mezzanine floor. Was glad they had kept the tiles on the walls and pillars. The view over the courtyard hardly changed. Except for the 1914–18 War Memorial. That was new. Well, new to her. Ivy had been in Russia since before then. Litvinoff was her married name.

Had met her husband when she was still a typist with the company and he was staying in a lodging house in the Farringdon Road, along with some other Russian exiles who have since become better known, including one called Leon Trotsky. Ivy became the wife of Max Litvinoff, the first foreign minister of the first socialist republic under Lenin. Had returned in her old age to spend her last years in her homeland. The company, though a pillar of capitalism had invited her to look around and the company magazine editor had thought it worth half a page. Very sporting, very British. Indeed at one point in the short article there was almost a note of pride in *our Ivy*.

Herbert M'Guigan, a Belfast man known familiarly as Herbie, nearly missed reading it and was indignant on that account. By Christ, he thought, our Ivy played with the big boys all right. And only half a page – but a whole page for the knickers dropping in the 1926 General Strike! He read with awe the bare catalogue of celebrated people Ivy must have known, the great historical events she must have witnessed from the inside. Herbie wished that everybody he subsequently met had also read and been equally impressed by the brief account of our Ivy, for he had in full measure all the Irish fondness for saying things that would go the rounds with his name on them, for coining memorable phrases of whatever truth or relevance or cost to reputations (did you hear what M'Guigan said about . . .).

'By Jesus,' he said to people to whom he pointed out the article, 'our Ivy got into the big league when she dropped *her* knickers.'

He did not make this remark to his wife, whose perusal of the company magazine concentrated upon the promotions, the mug shots of the promoted, their brief biographies and office careers, and their ages, especially their ages. His wife would wonder bitterly at Herbie letting them keep him back for so long, which prevented him from inviting her to laugh at the joke he had made at the lunchtime drink to celebrate one of the promotions. He said that he had worked out that he was two hundred and fifty-sixth in the line of succession to the

General Manager, and that it needed only two hundred and fifty-five simultaneous deaths for M'Guigan to have to don the crown, assume supreme power; it was a sobering thought.

In fact Herbie was not as easy-going about being passed over for promotion as his desire to uphold his country's reputation for wit and humour might have suggested. He had been privately displeased by the way in which the young actuary whose promotion they were celebrating had arrogantly dismissed the idea that reaching Herbie's rank at Herbie's age was in any sense an achievement. You had to get to that rank by thirty at the latest if you were to get anywhere, the young pup said, and the ambitious young men had all nodded vigorous agreement. The pup had coolly assessed the chances of success. The problem of getting to the top is the problem of *getting out of the middle*. Most people get stuck in the middle. Everywhere. Every big organisation. Companies. Catholic Church. Politics. Easy enough to get to the middle but getting out of it . . .

Easy! Herbie had had to wait till he was fifty to get to where that pup was at twenty-seven. On the way back from the drink Herbie consoled himself with satisfying recollections of other young pups who, over the years, had swiftly passed him on the promotion ladder, the youngest-ever this or that, rising young men tipped for higher things. But. The years had passed. No longer the youngest-ever this or that. Overtaken by new youngest-evers. Rising stars that quickly waned.

He took a short-cut along a carpeted corridor lined with doors on which were names that might have served to illustrate the elusiveness of the glittering prizes. The names of rising young men and men who had been that once, the names of old has-beens and one or two burnt-out cases, now on the bottle. He was so preoccupied by this train of thought that he took a turning to the left instead of the right and found himself on Management corridor: wide; oak-panelled; deep-carpeted; furnished with luxurious armchairs in which those who came deferentially seeking finance could wait in the almost religious hush and anxiously rehearse their pleas. For factories. For film studios. For stage plays. For ingenious inventions. For wildest dreams.

His plastic cup of coffee was very hot. Herbie transferred the cup to his other hand to let his fingers cool. In doing so the cup slipped. He not only failed to stop it but somehow knocked it against one of the mahogany doors with a carved portico before it spilt on the carpet. It was the office of the General Manager.

Herbie waited aghast for the door to open. His office career floated swiftly before his mind's eye the way drowning men are said to see their whole lives again before they go under. Collector up the Shankhill in Belfast . . . a tanner a week on the auld aunt . . . the Friday pay night dash round the houses before they spent it . . . under the mangle with the coal man's money . . . take out a wee endowment . . . Belfast Divisional Office . . . a likely lad like you . . . the insurance exams . . . a contract is an agreement freely entered into by two or more parties to do or to withhold from doing . . . London Chief Office . . . marriage . . . mortgage . . . children . . . middle age.

Nothing happened. The stately door with the coffee dripping down it remained shut, the silence unbroken, the opulent corridor deserted. Herbie walked boldly out of the swing doors, swinging his arms in a manner the very opposite of furtive or guilty, and then turned sharply down a flight of picturesque winding stairs with a wrought-iron balustrade which had once been for menials to bring up coals for the managers' fires or sherry for their elevenses but was now merely a short-cut to the lower floors. He was safe.

As his inner agitation faded away he thought it almost a pity that nobody had witnessed the event and seen the way he emerged from the swing doors and could relate how . . . *the bold M'Guigan never turned a hair.* He bumped into several cronies with whom he resisted the temptation to breathe a word, swapping some tidbits of gossip instead about who had not been promoted though in expectation and how badly they were taking it. One of these chats took place near where the young actuary who had thrown the drinks party was conversing with a young woman seated at her desk. She had probably just resumed wearing very short skirts after a spell in trousers and had forgotten to close her legs again, reminding Herbie and his crony of something else besides promotion that they had not had their fair share of. The young man said something to the girl that made her laugh and Herbie felt keenly, as did his pal, all the resentful suspicions of older men that younger men were getting more of it than *they* ever did.

A figure suddenly hurried past them, half-running. It was one of the Senior Actuaries. Even the least discerning could recognise the nature of that run. It meant that he had been summoned abruptly to a higher presence. He passed another of his kind who was strolling unconcernedly in the opposite direction and addressed him urgently over his shoulder. People nearby caught the words, 'yes, *all* of us, *now*,' which had the effect of causing the leisurely stroller to turn about and hasten after his colleague with an equally grave demeanour. Something was up. There was a panic on.

Excited speculation broke out among the clerks on the nature of the panic, some of it ribald, some serious, ranging through the lavatorial, the venereal, the infantile, the sober, the dull, the sensational. It was the last which gained ground as people phoned friends and colleagues round Chief Office. The Chairman clubbed senseless by the wine waiter . . . The Chief Actuary kicked in the vestibule by a disgruntled policy holder . . .

Herbie's crony, Bert Green, refused to be caught up in the excitement. He had seen office panics before. Probably just a bit of protocol. Herbie and he agreed you wouldn't credit the panic there could be over a bit of protocol, and do you mind the panic when they put a new Junior Actuary into an empty Senior Actuary's office till his own was ready, you can see into a Junior Actuary's office with the glass panels but not a Senior Actuary's, there was such a hullabaloo they took the door off the hinges to defuse the crisis. Yes, yes. Probably somebody has got a bit of carpet or a leather armchair he's not entitled to. They'll never change human nature in this office during our time, Herbie and Bert said to each other.

When Herbie eventually got back to his desk there was a message on it to see his boss Mr Barnes *immediately*. Ronald Barnes was a contemporary of Herbie's and Herbie had known him in humbler days as Ron Barnes. This made it difficult for Ron to get Herbie to start addressing him as Mr Barnes as the latter would have wished, and he had to settle for a compromise. He said to Herbie, 'Take a seat, Herbert,' and Herbert said to him in his still-broad Belfast accent, 'What about ye, Ronald?'

Mr Barnes said very gravely that an extremely serious incident had occurred which he and his colleagues had been instructed to investigate. Any light that Heads of Department could throw upon the matter would be treated in the strictest confidence. *There had been an attack upon the General Manager.*

'A missile,' Mr Barnes said slowly and solemnly, 'was thrown.'

Herbie was visibly shaken by this news and his agitation was not helped by the pause which Mr Barnes felt necessary in order to let the enormity of the incident sink in.

'A cup of coffee was thrown at his door,' Mr Barnes said gravely, 'presumably intended for Mr Uckfield.'

'Get away,' said Herbie, impressed, 'just as well he didn't answer the door.'

'Yes indeed. It had been hurled *with considerable force* by a person or persons unknown, possibly a disgruntled member of staff following the recent staff review. The Staff Manager has just seen all the Junior Managers . . . '

'Get away,' interrupted Herbie eagerly, inviting a confidence that would go no further, *just between these four walls*, 'he thinks it might be one of the Junior Managers . . . '

'Certainly not,' said Mr Barnes, 'now if we could just go through your staff . . . '

'You'll find nobody like that in my department, Ronald,' said Herbie, a little hurt at the idea. It was true that some of them were demanding to see Mr Barnes and that you're going to get an earful, Ronald, Herbie conceded, but he said it was nothing compared to some departments. He had just been having a word with Bert Green and you'd feel sorry for him.

One promotion, he was allocated, between the lot of them. One! Would have been better with none at all. Has their wives on the phone! 'Herbie,' he says to me, says he, 'I'm not safe walking the streets at night!'

'Yes. *Your* department, Herbert. I have the reviews here . . . '

'Then there's the change of life,' said Herbie, 'there's a lot of it about. Bert Green had a terrible time.'

'What. How could Mr Green . . . '

'The wife,' said Herbie sternly, 'the wife. "Herbie," he says, "if they don't come and take *her* away, they'll come and take me away."'

'Starting with the Grade Twos,' said Mr Barnes, studying the papers.

'These young actuaries,' said Herbie, 'all that studying. Bound to be some breakdown with the strain. Young Evans was saying to me at his lunchtime drink, sure you were at it yourself, did you not hear him, if he hadn't got to Grade Six by twenty-seven he might have done himself harm. I says to him, says I, "Success can be dearly bought . . . "'

'Croker. J.,' said Mr Barnes very firmly, 'forty-two years old, unlikely to go further . . . '

'And that funny-looking fella with the computer lot. The one with the shaved head and the beard squared off like a spade, you'd think he had his head on upside down. I think I'll pass the word round to keep an eye on him for you, Ronald.'

'No, no,' said Mr Barnes, alarmed, 'he's IBM. One of their top software specialists. From Sacramento.'

'California, eh?' said Herbie. 'Where they have those weird religions, animal sacrifice, naked women, you name it. Oh, I'll get him watched for you, Ronald, never you fear.'

'No, Herbert. We don't want you to do that,' cried Mr Barnes.

'Ah, sure it's no trouble,' Herbie said obligingly, 'I'll see that somebody follows him when he goes to the coffee machine from now on. For his own good. He might need help, Ronald, the man might need treatment.'

'No!' Mr Barnes shouted. He half-rose to his feet, still

shouting. Then he realised that shouting like that could look very bad and that Herbie was gazing at him with a sympathetic concern in which there was a tacit assurance that this would go no further, would stay between these four walls . . .

A little later Herbie left Mr Barnes's office, feeling it a pity that his behaviour could not be told and recounted (the bold Herbie . . . cheek of a regiment . . . no flies on M'Guigan). He looked in on his friend Archie who always had an *Evening Standard* and for a while sat studying the horses. Archie was a small weatherbeaten Junior Actuary, getting on in years, whose pastime of gambling was perhaps surprising in one who belonged to a profession concerned with the realistic calculation of probabilities. As Herbie studied form, Archie pursued his solitary occupation of sifting the medical statistics of death in order to arrive at more refined estimates of the human lifespan than the biblical three score and ten, especially in certain classes of people, such as publicans. It was no use the landlords of licensed premises writing in asking what was this about an extra premium for *impaired life* and swearing blind they did not sample the wares with unwise frequency. Archie could have echoed the famous reply that the First World War General of plebeian origin gave to Lloyd George: *'E 'ad 'eard different*. Herbie's eye suddenly caught the name of a horse.

'Hey, Archie,' he cried, 'I've got a tip. *Our Ivy*. At Newmarket on Saturday. Name of Jesus. Our Ivy!'

But he had to explain to him about Ivy Litvinoff. There was a copy of the company magazine in Archie's wastepaper-basket and he retrieved it. As Archie read the article sparks sometimes flew from the tip of his cigarette as it glowed red in the stream of oxygen he coughed past it. He was the only person Herbie knew who could hold a fag with one side of his mouth and cough with the other, spraying ash over his papers in doing so. Herbie wondered sometimes if in the name of Jesus Archie played the piano like that in the Musical Society. Archie was a brilliant classical pianist and had once given a concert in the Wigmore Hall. It was hard not to imagine him with a fag in his mouth coughing ash over the keys, but he must have been young once. As Archie read, Herbie thought of people in the company who might have had quite other careers: singers; astronomers; botanists; actors; athletes; he thought of the young people who would tell you they had joined the company because of its playing fields, running tracks, its small theatre, as well equipped as the smaller West End ones, and would hint at futures confidently dreamed.

Archie finished reading about our Ivy. He was a phlegmatic character and had few words.

'I'll try a fiver,' he coughed, 'how about you?'

Herbie considered. Normally it would have been such a small sum that he would not have to account for it to the wife. But this was different; he was not sure why. Something to do with an insurance book on the Shankhill; an old lady on the Farringdon Road looking for where a lodging house had been; the storming of the Winter Palace.

'Ah, to hell,' said Herbie, 'I'll have a fiver too.'

As Archie spoke on the phone to put a tenner on Our Ivy, Herbie absent-mindedly began humming a well-known air. It was 'The Internationale'.

The Willis Affair

Mr Willis was a Principal Clerk with the Bulwark Assurance Company and he drank pink gins at lunchtime. The few barmen in the City pubs who knew about pink gins would ask him 'in or out' as was proper, though most did not, and would serve him an 'in' automatically. If someone in the lunchtime drinking school asked what it meant, Mr Willis was very pleased to explain that 'out' – which only the expert barmen would know about – meant merely wetting the glass with the Angostura bitters and shaking out the surplus before adding the gin. But no use asking for it. If they didn't ask you it meant they didn't know.

'But does it make any difference?' he might be asked, especially by one of the office girls whom Mr Willis liked to invite to his lunchtime drinks to liven up the drinking school.

'Only a very little,' he would concede, 'though there are still a few of us about who can tell.'

'Oh, I love the way it goes all pink,' said Miss Mooney, the systems analyst who was computerising Impaired Lives next door to Mr Willis's Unsettled Deaths (Ireland), and was very attractive, putting all the men on their mettle.

'You do mean my gin?' said Mr Willis slyly, and then gave his famous little laugh like a sneeze that went not ha-ha but hatch-hatch, and his famous little jump backwards to express being startled or amused. Mr Willis was a familiar lunchtime figure in several of the City public houses and always held his glass of pink gin throughout, never resting it on bars or ledges, even when he did his little taken-aback jump of amusement or surprise in seeming sudden realisation of a *double entendre* in something he had just said. He was a small round man with a large head. 'That little man with no neck,' the typing pool would say when they couldn't remember his name, 'the one that got Sandra all tiddly on St Patrick's Day.' It was one of Mr Willis's little foibles to sport an enormous sprig of shamrock on St Patrick's Day. The internal mailing system would distribute large numbers of slips of paper that said: 'Pat Willis will be wetting the shamrock in Henekey's Long Bar from 11.30 a.m. onwards and hopes you can come.'

His habit of inviting pretty girls to his lunchtime drinks caused talk, especially if they were inexperienced drinkers and came back giggling and excited along with what was referred to as the 'hard-core' who stayed till closing time and came back making a lot of noise in the corridors, still swapping stories of office life and past times: who had got on and who had not; of cheek, push, charm, luck; of the war and their part in it; of lodgings they had stayed in when on company audits; of a Bulwark District Office next door to a junk shop that had a window full of second-hand false teeth.

Mr Willis's senior lady clerk, Miss Truft, sometimes spoke of going over his head about encouraging girls to take part in heavy lunchtime drinking. She several times raised the matter obliquely at meetings of the Ladies' Staff Welfare under 'Any Other Business', but without naming names so that the discussion tended to miss the point and to degenerate into gossip about the state some of the managers came back in. There was Mr Williamson, the boss of the lady chairman of the LSW, who spoke of him so often with a mixture of exasperation and affection that they all felt they knew him intimately. Mr Williamson had a great head of hair for his age, a thick grey mane. He had fine blue eyes and pale regular features. He wore little gold half-glasses which enabled him to look both shrewd and benign, sometimes even fatherly, especially with the typists and punched-card girls, whom he addressed as 'my dear' or even 'my dear child'. He usually had wine with his lunch and was even more fatherly in the afternoons. When the girls had to go into his office to do his filing they tried to go in pairs and got quite heated with each other over whose turn it was.

'Olive never goes so she doesn't.'

'I went with you last time.'

'Just wait till you want *me* to go with *you*.'

'Well stand at the door then.'

Mr Williamson was served tea in the afternoon in china that was distinctively superior to the plain cups of the staff and the Bulwark coat of arms was on it in blue, though on the other hand it was not quite so fine as the Senior Management's china on which the coat of arms was in red. Mr Williamson would lie back in his chair behind his desk with his chin on his breast and twinkle his eyes over his gold half-glasses.

'Well now, my dear,' he would beam kindly. Sometimes he slopped his tea in the saucer. When the lady chairman of the LSW told him that the father of one of the punched-card girls had died he had just come back from lunch.

'Oh poor child,' he cried out, 'send her to me so that I can cuddle her.'

'At least he doesn't ply them with strong drink,' said Miss Truft, trying to get the matter back to the point, 'unlike *some*.'

'Good heavens no,' said the lady chairman of the LSW, 'Mr Williamson is a gentleman.'

Then came the awful scandal of the Christmas party held by Unsettled Deaths (Ireland). Miss Truft would never forget it till her dying day. Indeed if Personnel had not put Miss Frobisher on to it Miss Truft would not have been able to do more than hint obliquely at what she had witnessed with her own two eyes in the Lady Supervisors' toilet. Miss Frobisher was a blunt no-nonsense woman who was expert in the questioning of women and girls on matters concerning the behaviour of men. Miss Truft had previously been enormously impressed on an occasion when she had taken three girls to see Miss Frobisher about a window cleaner who, they said, hung about the doors to the Ladies' Rest Room. The girls had not been able to tell Miss Truft exactly what he was doing but Miss Frobisher adopted a brisk questioning method whereby they needed only to say yes or no or even just nod or shake their heads when it came to the use of certain words, the specifying of acts, the naming of parts.

After the Christmas party affair it was Miss Truft herself who was questioned by Miss Frobisher in this manner, though of course being an older woman – who had been in the Land Army during the war – she was at least able to speak the term *sexual intercourse* quite firmly and to insist that the blame be put where it lay: with the Head of Department, Mr Willis. She would come to the Lady Supervisors' toilet in a minute, she told Miss Frobisher, refusing to be rushed. She really must be allowed to tell the full story of how it started. It was when the Ladies' Staff Welfare Committee arrived for a drink of Miss Truft's damson wine and a mince tart. She was actually pouring the drinks when Mr Willis and Mr Howard butted in. Miss Truft was in no doubt as to why. It was because of Miss Mooney. Miss Truft said that she really did not know why Miss Lee and Miss Vernon had brought her along, as Impaired Lives had their own party – and knowing Mr Willis! Mr Willis and Mr Howard made a beeline for Miss Mooney the moment they saw her, and started plying her with strong drink. Miss Truft became excited as she spoke. Mr Howard snatches the glass of my damson wine out of Miss Mooney's hand and says, 'You won't want that, dear,' and then throws it out of the window! Mr Willis thinks this is very funny. He has this paper hat on. Such rudeness! My damson wine came second in Arts and Crafts two years running. But before I could say anything *all* the men are gathered round. Helping her to my mince tarts. Pulling her cracker for her. Putting her funny hat on for her. Mr Willis shouting that he saw her first and pretending to beat them back with that Irish shillelagh club thing he uses as a paper weight. And then the stories! How he and Mr Howard won the war between them! And when Miss Truft spoke of her experience with the bull when she was in the Land Army Mr Willis made a quite awful joke which even some of the men thought he should have kept for the saloon bar. Then there was the 'in' or 'out' carry-on with the pink gin. Quite, quite disgraceful, and Miss Truft wished particular note to be made of it on Personnel's report. All that blindfolding and seeing if Mr Willis and then Miss Mooney could tell if it was 'in' or 'out'. At one stage they had a whole row of glasses of gin. Leading Miss Mooney up to them blindfolded. Mr Howard shouting that spitting out was not allowed. Some of the others just as bad. But all taking their cue from our Head of Department, Mr Willis. And when they unwrap their presents from the Christmas tree what do you think Mr Willis gets? A breathalyser! Mr Howard thinks it very funny to read the instructions as though he's chanting a psalm in church. Even some of the men took a dim view. What drink does to men is a revelation. Miss Truft was quite relieved when Miss Mooney went off with some of the younger ones – though no one could possibly have guessed!

It was at this point that Miss Frobisher had to help Miss Truft describe what she had seen, by means of down-to-earth questioning. Miss Truft had gone to the Lady Supervisors' toilet at the request of Security who were starting to clear the office. Where was Mr Willis? Oh, he was shouting about last orders and drinking-up time and his shillelagh and his breathalyser. Wouldn't let Mr Howard blow into it. But would let Miss Mooney blow into it and nobody else. Such a carry-on for grown men – let alone a Head of Department. And such shouting and sniggering the pair of them, about how Miss Mooney could tell whether it was 'in' or 'out'. Quite, quite disgusting. Should be laid before Management! Would never have been allowed before computers. Miss Truft thought computers had a lot to answer for, though it was no excuse for Mr Willis. But the toilets. What *actually* had she seen? Miss Mooney. Miss Truft had seen Miss Mooney. And? And Mr Clarke. Who would have thought it! Such a nice young man! Married only last year. That quiet little girl from Lapses and Surrenders. Brought the baby up to show us only last month. Shocking! Miss Truft had knit it a pair of bootees. Appalling! And had the Security man seen them? Oh no. Miss Truft had cried out to him not to go in. Miss Frobisher said this was a pity, but Miss Truft said that she couldn't possibly . . . let a *man* see . . . Here Miss Truft was determined to show that it was not a silly young girl Miss Frobisher was dealing with but a mature woman, so she said very distinctly, 'They were engaging in sexual intercourse.' Was Miss Truft quite sure? And Miss Truft said sharply that she hadn't been two years in the Land Army during the war for nothing! The only question was whether the girl had been a victim of Mr Willis plying her with strong drink! But Miss Frobisher made her spell out exactly what she had seen, just as if she was a young girl, with her relentless series of questions. Yes to this. No to that. On the floor? No. Against the wall? Yes. Undressed. No. So it was from the posture and the movements? Yes. Were his buttocks moving? Yes. In and out? Yes.

Miss Truft's cheeks had burned so hotly under this catechism that there were spots of colour in them for hours afterwards. She was almost relieved when Miss Frobisher had her over the next day to sign the Discussion Report of their conversation and said that both Miss Mooney and Mr Clarke had confirmed that Miss Truft had seen what she thought she had seen. 'And has she . . . no complaint?' 'None,' said Miss Frobisher. 'But surely . . . ' said Miss Truft. Miss Frobisher consulted a piece of paper that looked very like another Discussion Report form. She read from it in a carefully neutral tone: 'says it was his birthday.'

'But she's got six A levels,' cried Miss Truft incredulously, 'she's taking the actuarial examinations.'

'Yes,' said Miss Frobisher evenly, in the tones of a woman whom nothing can shock, 'there's a meeting arranged about it. Mr Willis and the LSW will be attending.'

The meeting was chaired by the new Personnel Manager who had only recently been promoted to the position following the retirement of his predecessor who had looked like Ewart Gladstone. The new man was very modern and had been on all the training courses for the managing of personnel, or *human resources*, as employees were now called. Men like Mr Willis were a great trial to him and he would be glad when all that generation retired, as they were an obstacle to the new human resources management methods being put into full effect: the evaluation of self-motivation factors, for instance. Mr Willis being non-progressive, that is he could not expect any more promotion, should have had a low-quartile self-motivation factor on his In-depth Appraisal Ratings – perhaps as low as two point eight – had the still-powerful rearguard of old-fogy managers not insisted that all Heads of Department must be given a high rating otherwise they wouldn't have been made Heads of Department. Well! Made nonsense of the Wardle-Schenck human resources index!

By the time this meeting took place Mr Willis had changed his attitude to the affair. At first he had gone about with a face like thunder, hinting at legal action for defamation of character over the stories that were being put about that it was he who had been found in the ladies' loo. One version had it that the girl had breathalysed him for being incapable! Even the typists sniggered over that one. 'That little man with no neck,' they sniggered, 'and that skinny computer girl that wears the latest goo-goo glasses and no bra.' But then he decided to change tack and to treat the stories as flattering, allowing his cronies to chaff him about it.

'Chance would have been a fine thing,' Mr Willis would shout back good-humouredly, doing his little taken-aback leap, perhaps pink gin in hand. 'Hatch-hatch,' he would laugh in mock breathless amazement. He adopted this line at the meeting called by Personnel in order to consider Miss Frobisher's report. The chairman of the Ladies' Staff Welfare Association later agreed with Miss Truft that Mr Willis had been allowed to turn the meeting into a farce. Asking for the figures for car-hire to take home girls who had passed out at the Christmas parties. And didn't Charlie Voles, the side-door porter, carry that fat girl from Personnel's own party to the Ladies' Rest Room? And couldn't Security tell a tale or two about clearing the building after the Christmas parties? And what a sight for sore eyes the Ladies' Staff Welfare Association would have encountered in the men's showers at the weight lifters' end of the gym, to say nothing of the Camera Club darkroom, the rifle range, the Christian Fellowship chapel. The Personnel Manager said he did not have the figures to hand but that they had not shown any marked increase over previous years. A large office of nearly 1,500 staff . . . compared very well with similar establishments in the City . . . voices raised to abolish office parties but should keep under review pro tem . . . provided no upward trend . . . perhaps certain comments should not be minuted . . .

'Must expect 1 per cent casualties,' cried Mr Willis, 'hatch-hatch.'

'Yes,' said the Personnel Manager vaguely, not certain quite what Mr Willis meant other than that it had something to do with war-time training for Alamein or D-Day or something like that.

'And so,' concluded Miss Truft bitterly, 'Mr Willis comes out of it smelling of roses.'

At lunchtime after the meeting Mr Willis alluded to the affair over a few pink gins and in such a way that showed it might eventually become a good lunchtime story, with a bit of editing and obscuring of names. A beautiful young computer person. A naughty married man. A spinster of a certain age . . . who could be made to seem very innocent and old maidish . . . thought the kiss of life was being administered and rang for the ambulance . . . and so on . . . and so forth. But Mr Willis had rather mixed feelings about some other versions which, until the office grew tired of it, continued to circulate through the company even as they grew more feeble, like spreading ripples on the surface of a pool, but reaching even distant regional offices before finally dying out.

'What's this I hear,' the Aberdeen manager boomed out at Mr Willis in the foyer of one of London's biggest hotels on the occasion of the Bulwark Annual Dinner, as hundreds of dinner-jacketed men streamed towards the banqueting hall, 'what's all this about you being pulled off some old tail at a company wine-tasting and breathalysed?'

'Old tail,' expostulated Mr Willis, 'hatch-hatch.'

The Bulwark Annual Dinner was a very big affair. There were no wives invited. The men sat at long tables, each with a letter above it indicating a region of the country. After the speeches some of the tables would break out into singing certain songs with an almost patriotic fervour, as if they were a kind of anthem with which to assert the honour of the region. Thus the Yorkshire contingent might succeed in getting 'Ilkley Moor' going vigorously after one or two false starts had petered out, and this might provoke the Belfast men to reply with 'When Irish Eyes are Smiling'. This rivalry was tolerated as an Annual Dinner tradition provided it did not go too far and get too rowdy. Some of the London Chief Office staff were appointed as table stewards on the regional tables and it was their duty to see that this did not happen, especially during the speeches from the top table which were expected to be heard with no more than the customary table-thumping and roars of laughter at the jokes. The table stewards were issued with little blue cards on which they were supposed to itemise shortcomings either in the service or the behaviour of the guests.

Mr Willis had been assigned to 'H' table as steward to the Belfast Division. Some of the Belfast men had clearly been drinking before they arrived and gave Mr Willis excited accounts of a wild night out on the town they had had away from their wives. There was much talk of Soho. Mention of Brewer Street set them off in a babble of admiring reminiscence of how they had lived it up.

'Your man Geordie here waltzes up to her . . . '

'The bold Hughie says to one of them, says he . . . '

Mr Willis listened sceptically. He knew that they would have gone about in groups, none of them daring to break ranks and go off on his own for fear word of it got back to the wife. Mr Willis had no sympathy with their eager desire to play up to the English idea of Irishmen being wild and colourful. Mr Willis knew that they were not in the least like that at home. Mr Willis had been seconded to the Belfast office for six months and knew that the reality was very different: the majority were conservative, sabbath-keeping, church-going. He would never forget – indeed it was one of his pink gin stories of the more astringent sort – how he had quite innocently caused himself to be snubbed, ostracised, treated as a moral outcast for . . . what? Breaking the Protestant Sunday! Mowing his landlady's lawn on the sabbath! So he rather brutally deflated their night-out-on-the-town account of themselves as roistering blades by cutting in with a remark that he thought rather good.

'Next thing is you'll be cutting your grass on a Sunday,' he said wickedly, 'hatch-hatch.'

Their table was very near a small stage on which a buxom soprano rendered a tasteful selection of German *leider* in a *very* low-cut gown. When one of the Belfast men expressed his appreciation by rising to his feet and clapping his hands together over his head very slowly and loudly Mr Willis took out his blue card and showed it to him in a way so like a football referee warning a player that the table choked in amusement. Not that Mr Willis wrote anything on the blue card. Mr Willis submitted a *nil return*. He nearly always did. Except that once when he got slightly splashed with gravy – years before.

Mr Willis circulated during the interval, having a word here and there with old acquaintances. He slipped away into the hubbub when another table steward, new to the game, approached him accompanied by one of the Belfast men from Mr Willis's table who had had something spilled over him by a waiter and thought that Mr Willis should take note of it.

Mr Willis was chaffed about the sex orgy at his Christmas party; told his story about the blue card warning, hatch-hatch, and the man with gravy down his flies, adding in a very serious tone that he always loved that moment when the doors to the kitchen swung open and the army of waiters and waitresses surged out each with a pile of plates, that moment when dozens of plates hit the tables simultaneously in a great CRASH-SH-SH . . .

'Bound to be 1 per cent casualties,' concluded Mr Willis, 'hatch-hatch.'

He sat down for a moment or two with a very senior manager who had very graciously greeted him in an unctuous, plum-in-the-mouth cockney accent which Mr Willis could imitate so successfully in his pink gin story of the clerk being reprimanded for wearing a tweed suit in the office

– tweed suits were all very well in their place, 'Wy, 'e 'imself wore one at weekends.'

'Will you tyke woine with me?' said the manager to Mr Willis very ceremoniously in his broad London posh, raising his glass as if some sort of sacrament were involved, splashing some red wine tipsily into two glasses.

When Mr Willis got back to his table he saw that the Belfast men had bribed the waiters to leave extra decanters of whisky and brandy for the speeches and after.

The principal speaker was Lord Telling, the great law-lord, Master of the Rolls. Mr Willis thought him a disappointment. Two of his three funny stories Mr Willis had heard before and the third was not, in Mr Willis's view, well told – Mr Willis said he thought somebody should book him for it on the blue card, hatch-hatch – but this did not stop the applauder of the soprano artiste's bosom from thumping the table so hard after everybody else had stopped that Mr Willis said that one more off-side and he would book him, hatch-hatch.

As soon as possible after the speeches Mr Willis made a surreptitious departure. He was supposed to stay for 'Auld Lang Syne' and 'The Queen', but that would have meant having to sit through all that awful chorusing of 'When Irish Eyes are Smiling' on 'H' table. Quick off the mark though Mr Willis was, he was however beaten to the cloakrooms above the banqueting hall by someone else, or rather by a cry on behalf of someone else that was passed from mouth to mouth among the flunkeys on the stairs. The cry was 'Lord Telling's hat'. The cry passed Mr Willis on the balcony and when he reached the counter of the cloakroom – on which imposing receptacles were being put out to receive the grateful offerings of the Bulwark Annual diners – the cry was starting back on its return journey, accompanied by the hat itself. A tall glossy black silk hat went sailing past him, spinning in the air, and he watched in amusement as it was caught by a flunkey and sent flying on its way towards the stairs. 'Lord Telling's hat, Lord Telling's hat.'

But Lord Telling's hat never reached the stairs. Even as Mr Willis received his coat he heard the cry change, take on a different note: consternation, dismay. *Lord Telling's hat!* Had somebody trampled on it? Dropped it in a slop bucket. That would teach them to play circus tricks with the hat of the Master of the Rolls! But when he went out on to the landing he was informed of what had happened by someone he knew well who was leaning on the balustrade gazing down into the hubbub below in the banqueting hall – into which the hat had fallen! His informant had such a noble hawk-nosed Roman Emperor's profile that he could well have been one of the dignitaries from the top table, except that Mr Willis knew him to be Charlie Voles, the side-door porter who carried girls who had had too much to the Ladies' Rest Room at the Christmas parties and who was present at the dinner only to perform menial duties. ''Ere,' he said to Mr Willis with evident satisfaction, 'that bleedin' nob's titfer went over the side. Somebody's in for a right bollocking. 'Ere,' Charlie Voles added excitedly, 'come and 'ave a look at this.'

But Mr Willis declined the invitation. The provocative singing challenges were beginning to be issued and taken up between tables. Those awful local songs. Mr Willis caught the faint sounds of 'Glasgow Belongs to Me'; 'Ilkley Moor'; 'The Floral Dance' in the medley of deafening chatter that drifted up among the cigar smoke. As he hurried to the stairs he noted that the Newcastle office seemed – for the moment – to be in the lead by getting their table into full throat with 'Blaydon Races':

. . . all with smiling faces
Ganging along the Scotswood Road

. . . and the word *road* was triumphantly prolonged in a great roar of ro-o-o-o-o-ad before the next line was emphasised with fists crashing down on the table:

To see the Blaydon Races.

He was well out of it. He hastened out into the bright lights of Park Lane, turning over in his mind several colourful items from the evening, which, with a bit of polishing, might make witty little pink gin anecdotes. No real gems among them but

. . . cutting your grass on Sunday . . . will you take wine with me . . . artiste's cleavage off-side warning with blue card. Not bad. And Lord Telling's hat. Mr Willis went home well pleased with himself.

Next morning seemed no different to Mr Willis from other mornings after previous Annual Dinners. Men with a normally loud and forceful presence seemed quiet and withdrawn, several faces in the corridors had a yellowish tinge to them. Mr Willis listened appreciatively to a rumour that the new Deputy Assistant General Manager – the youngest ever – had just had to go home in a taxi he was so unwell, it being his first year on the top table and nobody had told him to drink sparingly and *save himself* for the private party afterwards in a suite of rooms, at which there was *high jinks* far into the night. Serve that pup right, they agreed! Too pushing by far! The big boys probably did it to teach him a lesson! Not all love and kisses among the big boys, hatch-hatch.

One or two people asked him what was this incident after the dinner that Personnel were looking into.

'What, people pissing in the street,' said Mr Willis, 'hatch-hatch.' On a previous Annual Dinner when Mr Willis had not sloped off early, but came out with the crowd, he had been startled to see a dinner-jacketed figure standing thoughtfully on the pavement with his hands on his hips and with great deliberation urinating copiously through the railings and down into the basement area of an expensive block of flats, quite indifferent to the stream of people stepping to one side to get round him.

'Probably one of my Irishmen,' said Mr Willis, 'hatch-hatch.'

Yes, they said, they thought it was. Personnel were reported to be taking statements behind closed doors.

'I await the call,' laughed Mr Willis, 'hatch-hatch.'

When he got back to his department he found that he had already had the summons. His desk was littered with bits of paper containing scribbled messages of increasing urgency. In case he did not notice these Miss Truft rushed at him to say with great satisfaction that he was wanted on Personnel *immediately*.

The red 'Do Not Enter' panel was on above the Personnel Manager's door when Mr Willis arrived and he had to wait till they phoned in first. He knew at once that it was something very serious, a quite different affair from the meeting about the Christmas party. Much more high-powered. The Personnel Manager was not in the chair. The chair was being taken by Mr Lipcott, the Deputy Assistant General Manager who was supposed to have gone home with a bad hangover. He looked very ill. Had it not been the morning after the Annual Dinner Mr Willis would have wondered if there was not something in the whisper going round that he was *not a well man*. The big boys were making him earn his promotion!

Mr Lipcott addressed Mr Willis as Willis.

'What do you know about this disgraceful business, Willis?' he said coldly.

Mr Willis tried the light-hearted approach by asking whether his Belfast men had been committing public nuisances 'after the ball was over' and gave his little laugh, hatch-hatch.

'The business of Lord Telling's hat,' said Mr Lipcott icily and snapped his finger at the Personnel Manager who hastily passed him a blue card from among a pile of them at his side.

''H' table. Belfast Division,' he read out. Willis had been steward on 'H' table had he not? This was his signature, was it not? He had submitted a nil return? *A nil return?* Nothing about Lord Telling's hat? And they all rolled their eyes in disbelief, gave little mirthless titters of bitter amusement, threw up their hands at each other in incredulity and despair. *A nil return for 'H' table!*

Mr Willis had to confess that he had sloped off early before the end. Did not feel up to . . . 'When Irish Eyes are Smiling' . . . you know how it is. Also he had had . . . and he made little rueful gestures with his hand and elbow of the glass-raising kind, which he instantly regretted when he saw Mr Lipcott's yellow suffering face gazing at him without sympathy. He thought it wiser not to mention having seen Lord Telling's hat whiz past him in the cloakrooms. He prayed that Charlie Voles would keep mum about trying to get him to look at what was happening to the hat down below . . . that must have been what he had been excited about. 'H' table had got hold of it! But what had they done with it? He tried to find out.

But that was what the enquiry was about. Since Mr Willis had deserted his post he could clearly be of no assistance in bringing to light the full facts and the identities of the culprits in a disgraceful incident which his presence might well have prevented. Mr Lipcott spoke these words as if reading them and Mr Willis knew they would appear in some kind of report.

'I am having to report to the board,' said Mr Lipcott. Mr Willis was in disgrace and no mistake. Before they dismissed him from their presence he managed to glean something of what had happened to Lord Telling's hat. Improper use made of it. Singing with it on! Passing it round to receive coins! And worse than coins . . . *a substance* . . . They would add no more to these ominous words. Had Lord Telling put it on . . . with . . . this . . . substance? Oh my God!

'You will make no attempt Willis, to contact any of 'H' table, either now or when they return to Belfast. The least said outside this room the better. You will not, Willis, discuss it with any of your staff or your peers.'

The Personnel Manager was pleased to see the term 'peers' which he had learnt on his Management courses – though in the form 'peer groups' and which he used in all his circulars and memos being taken up by Management. In Mr Willis's case it meant his drinking cronies of the same rank. The other senior men in the room all muttered with shudders of horror that they did not want the press to get hold of it. They murmured gravely about the *Company Image* being damaged. 'No gossiping, Willis,' he was exhorted sternly as he left the room. *The Image of the Company*.

Mr Willis took this admonition more seriously than some people would have thought, given his reputation as a hard-core pub-lunch man with a fund of funny stories and no prospects career-wise. He really was a company man at heart. His father had been a District Manager. He had been recruited during the depression of the 1930s when only those with relatives in the company were taken on. There were other Willises around. The Willises were a 'Bulwark family'. Mr Willis's usual escapades and obstreperousness were not much more than a kind of little-boy naughtiness almost designed to test and confirm the reassuring existence of a mildly disapproving but at the same time all-embracing authority that regulated and enfolded his life like a warm womb. Those who expected him to regale the lunchtime drinking schools with a well-told story of the Annual Dinner affair were disappointed when he dutifully played it down.

The office as a whole was not so easily put off, and for days it was agog to hear the latest account of what was going on behind closed doors to which people were being summoned but would say nothing. So many 'Do Not Enter' signs were glowing red on Management corridor that it gave rise to jokes about the 'red-light district'. So much rumour was flying about that it seemed inevitable that the press would get wind of it. The board even considered holding an extra ordinary meeting.

But then the danger passed. The stories that were going the rounds were so different that they were contradictory and so wildly wide of the mark as to produce a reaction of scepticism. Clerks who were not quite senior enough to be invited and who therefore thought that the Annual Dinner should be abolished refused to be impressed by the most lurid accounts and murmured nonchalantly with a blasé smile that it sounded like the usual shenanigans. Standard form, old man. About par for the course, old chap. A bit much old Willis submitting a nil return on his blue card, they conceded, when the Irish were doing a striptease to slow hand-claps, but there you are. What about that year when MacDonald of Cashiers turned up in a kilt and got it ripped off him?

Miss Truft would have liked to believe all of the most sensational of the stories but reluctantly had to settle for one. In the one that she chose to relate excitedly to anyone who would listen, Lord Telling's high office was variously confused with that of the Lord Chief Justice or the Lord Chancellor. Miss Truft liked the sound of Lord Chancellor. The Lord Chancellor, Miss Truft recited. They say . . . insulted by your Mr Willis and the Irish . . . *and* his lady wife. Oh yes. Miss Truft said *your* Mr Willis to her colleagues on the Ladies' Staff Welfare who thought she was a bit hard on the little man. A row of the Irish lined up against the railings. *Your* Mr Willis the ringleader. Letting fly through it. Like dogs. As the Lord Chancellor and his lady wife came up the steps! At this point Miss Truft almost wished it had been the Lord Chief Justice, from some association with sentencing and handing down of terms of imprisonment and so on, but a *lady wife* didn't somehow suit him so well. The Lord Chancellor's lady wife offered the run of Bond Street with a blank cheque to replace her lovely gown. 'Your Mr Willis will go no further in this company,' said Miss Truft with a quiver of the hips.

A few months later Unsettled Deaths was addressed by The Way Ahead Task Force Team. They were to be computerised. At one point the clever young man from Computers said that what might seem a minute to ordinary people was 60,000 milliseconds to *them*, which so over-awed the ladies that they did not dare to ask any questions during the 'Any Questions' session and they rather thought Mr Willis a bit obstreperous – it was after a noisy return from lunch – when he said with that laugh of his like a sneeze that what might seem a gallon to ordinary people was eight pints to *him*, hatch-hatch.

At a meeting on Personnel with the red light on they decided what to do with Mr Willis and the ladies of Unsettled Deaths.

All of them except two were to be transferred. Mr Willis and Miss Truft to be retired early. Would find it difficult to adjust. All that 'peer group' of war-time 'returnees' found it hard to adapt to the computerisation programme. Also the Human Resources Evaluation programme. Would have to let them go. The Personnel Manager searched his memory for a phrase he had heard somewhere to do with this kind of situation. When people got caught up in events. Omelettes? Breaking eggs? No. He had it now.

'Bound to be a few casualties,' he said, 'we have to allow for 1 or 2 per cent casualties.'

A Grounding in the Classics

He was a very impressionable boy, and full of imagination. The story in their class reader of the Gorgon Medusa with snakes for hair whom it was death to look upon except in the reflection of a burnished shield appealed to him very strongly. Eagerly he pointed out Medusa-like girls with curls or ringlets and would shield his eyes in horror or go rigid as if struck down dead. He tried to start a street game which involved advancing backwards upon girls like big Cissie who had a mop of ginger curls, while gazing into a bin lid. He tried to get big Cissie nicknamed Gorgon, but to his annoyance they started calling *him* Gorgon instead, despite his angry protests. He was particularly angry with Bertie Marlow over the Gorgon affair. Sly Bertie had led him on, had pointed out big Cissie to him, had even suggested the bin lid, and then had turned round and led the campaign to get people to nickname him Gorgon. Hello Gorgon. Here comes the bold Gorgon. Lend us your comics Gorgon. So assiduously did sneaky Bertie Marlow *Gorgon* him that it caught on for a while and lasted long enough for it even to take wing like some windborne seed over the school walls into the streets beyond, where, however, it suffered a slight mutation to *Gordon*. Years later, his mother would sometimes be puzzled by people who knew them only slightly referring to him as Gordon and when she mentioned this he would remember that school reader with its stories of the gods and half-gods, not only of the Greeks but of the Norsemen, of

Valhalla and Wodin and Thor, of the half-god Loki the troublemaker, patron of slyness and treachery. He tried to get sly Bertie Marlow nicknamed Loki, though in vain. Not because of the Medusa affair. It was because of the affair of the frog.

There was another story in that reader about a big mechanical frog made by a poor clockmaker. It could jump over a city wall at dead of night with soldiers inside it to rescue a beautiful princess from her wicked uncle.

'We have one of them at home, Gorgon,' whispered Bertie Marlow at him from the desk behind. What was more, if Gorgon went home with them after school, he could have it.

'Get stuffed,' he whispered back derisively. The Marlows lived in the railway cottages near the goods sidings where there were no beautiful princesses, muskets, drums. He did a two-fingered gesture behind his back, which is not as easy as it sounds.

'Honest,' whispered Bertie, and followed this at intervals with, 'Cross my heart,' 'May God strike me blind,' and other attestations to truthfulness, some of them so fearful in the penalties invoked that it was impossible not to be somewhat impressed.

'Ask Ned,' said Bertie. Ned was his elder brother.

At break in the playground Bertie led him over to Ned for confirmation.

'Certainly we have,' said Ned scornfully, as if angry with his brother for caring who believed it or not.

'It come off a fairground,' he added in an indifferent take-it-or-leave-it tone that insidiously undermined disbelief.

Fairground. So he was not being asked to swallow fifes, drums and princesses? His interest quickened, in spite of the too obvious pleasure on Bertie's smiling face at having aroused it. When Ned with brutal candour said dismissively that it was only a two-seater, the reduction in scale, far from being a disappointment, on the contrary helped along the process of being persuaded that there might be something truthful in it after all.

Bertie placed his hand about three feet from the ground and

said, 'It could jump that height with Gorgon in it, couldn't it, Ned?'

'Away to hell,' said Ned angrily, though not to contradict, far from it. He gestured impatiently at the playground wall. 'It could clear that bloody wall, so it could.'

'And Gorgon can have it,' Bertie prompted, 'can't he, Ned?'

'Him or anybody else,' said Ned, impatiently turning away, 'first come, first served.'

Bertie watched triumphantly as scepticism melted away and was replaced by eagerness to acquire so delectable a possession.

When they reached the railway cottages after school, Mr Marlow was digging his garden in his railway clothes, still wearing bicycle clips. His bicycle was against the window. Mr Marlow was famous for being inseparable from his bicycle. He went everywhere on it, even to the public house. When he rode his bicycle home from the public house he pedalled so slowly that the bicycle nearly came to a stop and he would be about to fall over when he would turn the wheel sharply and start pedalling again just in time. People said it was like an act in a circus. Circus. Fairground. Two-seater. The association was irresistible and exciting. He greeted Mr Marlow with unusual warmth.

'Hello Gordon,' said Mr Marlow as Bertie and Ned went in to carry out the frog.

The curtains moved at the window along the sash of which was a row of little ornaments. He saw a hand do something to them. Then Bertie and Ned appeared. Bertie watched him smilingly as Ned, with an ironical bow, handed him a small object. It was a little delft frog on which it said 'Present from Portrush'.

Quite gravely he accepted it, turned and walked away. Only when he was out of their sight did he give vent to his disappointment and rage. Rage at himself for being made gullible by acquisitiveness. Rage at Bertie Marlow. He turned down an alleyway alongside the playground wall of his school. There was no one about.

'Fuck you,' he shouted, 'fuck you, Bertie bloody Marlow. Fuck you, *Loki* Marlow, fuck the lot of you.'

He hurled the little seaside gewgaw high into the air. It sailed over the school wall at almost the very point where Ned had said it could clear the wall with him in it.

He was allowed a single moment of mollifying satisfaction before the sound – musical almost – of breaking glass filled him with horror. He nearly started to run wildly in panic, till he remembered just in time that no one had actually *seen* him do it. He emerged from the alleyway composing his features into that sweet angelic look which had served him so well in the past – even with his mother, sometimes – and might, with a bit of luck, see him through this latest affair in perfect innocence.

Mr Bunting

The radio played very loudly all day long in the recreation room of the admission ward of Antrim Mental Hospital which, until recent times, had been known as the County Asylum. Mr Bunting would have liked the radio to be turned down a little. He was used to the much quieter atmosphere of the place he had come from: a well-known nursing home for elderly incurables of the better class who were still able to get about.

On his second day in Antrim he spoke in a gentle and courteous tone to one of the male nurses about the volume of the wireless. The male nurses had formerly been known as warders and still wore blue serge uniforms with peaked caps. The nurse told him curtly not to be selfish but to show consideration for others who might want to hear the wireless and Mr Bunting, who was not an argumentative man, did not like to point out that he had meant only when none of the other patients were listening to it – or at least seemed not to be, for of course with one or two it was hard to tell.

A little while later he happened to be the only patient in the recreation room, for he was the only one whose movements – for the present at least – were confined to the ward. He was examining the radio to see if he could find the knob that would turn down the volume when two of the male nurses rushed towards the set. There was a big football match on in England. They turned it up so loud it made the windows rattle and when the team they favoured scored a goal they yelled in jubilation and smacked their fists into their palms with great violence. When their excited eyes wandered to Mr Bunting, though without taking him in, he tried to smile to show he didn't really mind and to hide the fact that he was once more comparing his present surroundings with the Johnson Memorial Home, for he was most anxious to create a good impression in case this might influence his subsequent fate.

The windows of the recreation room had a wire grille over them through which he could see people walking about outside, most of them people from the other wards of the hospital. People were sent on to these wards from admission ward, if, that is, they were not allowed to go home, which, in Mr Bunting's case, would have been the Johnson Memorial Home. Many of the men he saw walking about wore coarse grey suits, ill fitting but hard wearing. Some shuffled along with blank dead faces, others on the contrary were filled with restlessness; no part of them was still, and rapid changes of expression reflected the frantic activity of their broken but whirring minds.

Mr Bunting, whenever he got the chance, spoke shyly but fondly of the Johnson Home, apologising for speaking without his teeth which had been left behind at the Home, and the lack of which made him leave uneaten some of the dishes that were put before him in the ward dining room where all the cutlery was carefully counted and locked up again after meals. 'Write to them to send on your teeth,' the male nurse would tell him sharply, and if Mr Bunting made light of it by saying that it might not be worthwhile as he would probably be going back very soon, the male nurse reminded him coldly that that wasn't for him to decide, whereupon Mr Bunting looked crestfallen.

One of the other patients was a rather nice young man whom Mr Bunting talked to about the Johnson Home. The young man was apt to flush a bright red and sweat profusely when people spoke to him. Another patient, who seemed to have the knack of overhearing doctors and nurses talking, said authoritatively that it was fear. It was fear that made him turn red and sweat like that. But he did not do it much with Mr Bunting, who in any case was not a person to be very frightened of. Mr Bunting told him all sorts of things about the Johnson Home, especially the things that some of the patients did which they were not supposed to do. Mr Bunting made the Johnson Home sound like a very jolly place where the bolder spirits got up to all sorts of pranks behind the matron's back.

When a certain song then much in vogue came on the wireless of the recreation room, 'In Eleven More Months and Twelve More Days We'll Be Out of the Calaboose', Mr Bunting smiled with pleasure for the first time. Why, he told the young man who sweated with fear, they had sung that at the Johnson Home Christmas Party. A group of them, of which Mr Bunting made it clear he had been a ringleader, had planned it as a prank. To their own words. 'In Eleven More Months and Twelve More Days We'll Be Out of the Johnson Home.' The matron and the visitors had taken it all in good part, and had, it seemed, even joined in. So well had it gone down in fact that Mr Bunting would not be surprised if they sang it next Christmas too.

At the end of his first week in admission ward Mr Bunting had a visitor, a Presbyterian minister, indeed one of those who had been a regular visitor at the Johnson Home and had joined in the singing of that song so good-humouredly. A male nurse, very respectful of the cloth, opened up a little room in the corridor for them to go into, locking and double-locking behind them the heavy main door of the ward. He also locked them into the little room using another of the great hoop of keys that hung from his belt.

The minister was carrying a small parcel, and it was quite evident from the strange filled-out look of Mr Bunting's face afterwards that this had contained his teeth. He put them straight in so as to be able to speak clearly and urgently, though in fact one of the first things he said was more in the way of polite conversation to the effect that the peace and quiet where they were was heaven after the noise of the ward, especially the wireless which never stopped.

The minister's visit gave Mr Bunting so much to think about that, notwithstanding having his teeth in, he hardly spoke a word between then and bedtime. So gloomy did he appear, that one of the other patients, the very same who knew why the shy young man sweated and blushed and who frequently claimed the distinction of being irrepressible in spirit and of always looking on the bright side, thought he would cheer him up by putting something hard under his mattress for a laugh. But the joke went wrong. Mr Bunting did indeed jump out of bed to see what it was but he did not join in the laughter. Far from it. He shouted at them that there was no fairness anywhere. None at all. Fairness was not to be hoped for in this world, he cried.

Later, deep in the night, those who slept badly – and most of them did not sleep well – heard cursing and sobbing which went on for a long time.

Next day Mr Bunting's absence from the recreation room was noticed by several of the patients and they asked each other where he was. The man who tried to cheer him up was able to inform them. He was one of those people who settle down very quickly in any institution and soon behave with easy familiarity concerning its ways, mastering in no time at all the local terminology for places, things, procedures, and able before long to tune in to the gossip. So he was able to name the ward that Mr Bunting had been taken to and said that he'd find a very different class of people there all right. He said this with a measure of satisfaction, for the way Mr Bunting had shouted at him still rankled.

'And what', another of them asked, 'about that place Bunting was forever bragging about, about the great time he had in the Johnson Home?'

'Surely,' put in the shy youth whom Mr Bunting had talked to more than the others, blushing a scarlet colour at the idea of being so bold as to speak up in company, 'surely he's going back there again?'

'No,' explained the cheerful one. 'They wouldn't have him back. He had tried to do himself in. They don't like that sort of thing at them places,' he assured them. 'They sent him his teeth with that clergyman with the word that they didn't want him back.'

A few minutes later the *Family Favourites* programme on the wireless played once more the song 'In Eleven More Months and Twelve More Days We'll Be Out of the Calaboose'.

Remembrance Day on Ivy Ward

The two-minute silence was observed on Ivy Ward as well as was possible considering that the patients were all old men with those ailments of old age which make stillness and silence very difficult even though, as they listened to the Remembrance Day ceremonies on their earphones, they tried to keep to a minimum their coughings; their restless turnings in bed; the chink of urine bottles against bed or locker. One of the old men was in a bad way, with screens round his bed, beside which sat his wife; his stertorous breathing was audible in the ward and from its monotonous regularity it was clear that he was unconscious.

When lunch was served an old man with a bottle of stout on his locker delayed starting to eat until he had managed to attract the attention of the woman at the dying man's bedside. He was worried in case the bottle of stout might upset her by its associations with mirth and merrymaking. He was anxious to let her know that there was no question of conviviality. He explained to her earnestly that he had one *every day*. He meant that it was his only remaining pleasure of the flesh and was of doubtful duration.

'Have your bottle of stout,' she told him. 'Mr MacDonald would have wanted you to have it.'

He was so grateful for her reassurance on the matter that when he caught her eye during his meal he half-raised his glass in her direction in an uncertain gesture of sympathy and she nodded back understandingly.

A young boy came into Ivy Ward from another ward nearby. He had been listening to the Remembrance Day poem on his earphones and the recital had moved him.

> They shall grow not old as we that are left grow old,
> Time shall not weary them nor the years condemn . . .

But it was the beauty of the words that the boy liked more than the meaning. He liked beautiful words, especially if they were sad. He liked being made sad by songs and poems. He enjoyed the sadness of the Remembrance Day poem as he had enjoyed the other requiem in his school reader with the lines:

> Home is the sailor, home from the sea
> And the hunter home from the hill.

He came in hoping that the old man with the bottle of stout would tell him more about the 1914–18 war. The old man had been with the Ulster Volunteers. He always spoke of going up to the front line as *going up the duckboards* and the boy had inferred that these were some kind of walkways laid down over the mud. The boy had listened the previous evening to a story about the duckboards. It had been prompted by the appearance on the ward of a black doctor, the first the old men had seen, though they had heard tell of brown ones in the Royal, and they had reminded each other of the Indians in turbans who used to go round the doors before the war carrying a roll of oilcloth that would last no time on your kitchen floor. The old man had said he was going up the duckboards with an officer when they met this black soldier that must have been from a Jamaican battalion. The officer had pushed the black fella off the duckboards just because he didn't get out of the way soon enough.

'Says I to him, says I, "Sir, the day will come, sir, when you'll not do that, sir."'

It seemed that the officer had put him on a charge, a young bugger of a lieutenant. 'He went up before the Captain and the Captain says, "What about this?" he says. "Did you say that?" he says, and says I, "Sir, I did, sir." Says he, "Don't let this happen again, next case please." That was all! When they marched him out the big sergeant said to him, said he, "Well done, Billy, that young bugger of a lieutenant will get one in the back if he's not careful!"'

The other patients had said nothing. Perhaps they had heard it before. But the boy had listened enthralled, catching a stirring glimpse of the stern military code: the being marched in and marched out on a charge; the bawling; the saluting; the feet stamping; the encouraging words of an escort whispered sideways on the move. He wanted to hear what happened next. The story seemed unfinished. The old man had merely concluded by repeating what he said to the officer on the duckboards, as if proud of its prophetic significance. But the boy wanted a tidier ending, a more dramatic one.

He had difficulty in conveying this as he waited for the old soldier to finish his stout, but finally he put the question straight. Had the young bugger of a lieutenant *got one in the back*?

'Hey. What?' said the old man, startled, even shocked. 'Ah no,' he went on sadly, 'he was killed not long after.' He said it thoughtfully, no longer speaking to the boy but to himself, remembering. 'And the sergeant. He was killed too. So was the Captain. Killed. They were all killed.'

The Carnivores

The speaker on 'The Irish in London' at the Kensington Historical and Literary Society had unfurled a map of London with the parts where the Irish were most concentrated coloured green. He drew attention to these areas with an ingenious telescoping pointer that he collapsed briskly to pocket size with a flourish, which, while it did not actually imply that he had invented it himself, did not deny it either – in rather the same way that if you wanted to infer that he was the first to discover where the Irish had principally settled in London he would not stop you from doing so. His biggest patches of green were in the vicinity of, or on the roads leading from, the northern railway termini, especially Paddington, at which the Irish had arrived on the boat-trains, especially during the nineteenth century.

After the lecture people lingered in the foyer chatting or fingering the publications offered on little stalls that had been set up to promote the aims of all sorts of societies and bodies, some to do with Irish affairs, some not. A very serious young man with a beard, near a Campaign for Nuclear Disarmament stall, was heard to give the earnest advice, seemingly based upon bitter experience, against employing leaflet printers who were not fully unionised, though whether this was in connection with Irish matters was not clear. An elderly man with an Ulster accent gesticulated with an upraised hand into which someone had pressed a leaflet, presumably promoting vegetarianism, headed in very bold type MEAT INFLAMES THE

PASSIONS. He was saying very heatedly that of course there must be separation of Church and State if the Protestants were ever to agree to a united Ireland, and later another of the same group, also clutching the tract against meat, said gravely that the Curragh Mutiny had posed the most serious threat to constitutional government in Britain since Pitt's bill on seditious utterances.

The connection between the London Irish and the great age of railways and steam was perhaps the reason for the stall furnished with mementoes such as tea towels on which were famous locomotives with names like Lord Palmerston or Duke of Wellington, and at which signatures were being collected to protest against the plans of a property company to knock down an engine shed designed by the great I.K. Brunel himself.

Stanley, a timid bookish railway clerk, stood about for a while, listening to these snatches of discussion all around him and wishing he was not too shy to join in. He would have liked to have been able to stand up at the meeting when it was thrown open for comment and say how very noticeable it was that many of the railway workers at Paddington station were Irish, though the foremen were mostly from the west of England. He would have liked to tell the man at the Railway Heritage stall that the carriage and wagon office where he worked had also been built by Brunel, and had a little cupola on top like a Wren church. He was quite a good mimic and, had he been able to push himself forward, could have made people laugh with imitations of Irish and West Country accents that he heard every day. He could have made a party piece out of the way his boss, Mr Trelford, a loud genial little Cornishman, shouted affably on the phone to colleagues down the line in Penzance, Reading, Bristol, Cardiff, Holyhead, or less affably debated with the many Irish cleaners, shunters, greasers under his command their foibles, shortcomings, excuses, urgent needs concerning lodgings, early rising, drink, money to send home to Ireland. But Stanley's timidity, while it might have allowed him to reproduce accurately enough the soft Irish shilly-shallying ('Sure, t'was the ould stomach, Mr Trelford, bad luck to it . . . when I turn on that side there's no waking me'), would have quite destroyed any likeness to little roaring Mr Trelford, whose portrait could have been rendered only with the bold loudness of the original: 'Oh ah m'dear! . . . well I be buggered! . . . oh ah my old beauty!'

On his way back to his lodgings Stanley found crumpled in his pocket a MEAT INFLAMES THE PASSIONS leaflet. *A peaceful world impossible as long as men are carnivores. Territorial aggressiveness. Domination. Lust.* When Stanley was a boy *lust* was one of the words that had given him a secret little thrill of excitement when he encountered it. His mother had once spoken to him about lust. Hoped he would always respect women. No excuse for lust. Should think of his mother and his sister. If men weren't encouraged. Hoped no woman would ever corrupt any son of hers. The word again stirred in him a little of that old excitement, now with wistfulness in it. He wondered, was it true what one of the Irish greasers had told him about Mr Trelford: that a lot of them owed him money and, if they could not repay it, they could, in lieu, send a wife or a daughter to visit him when he worked late . . . Surely not? Stanley had queried, shocked. And *daughters*? Ah sure some of them fellas would have six of them, he was assured, half in pity, half in contempt. The Irish in London speaker had said that Ireland's principal export was people. Male brawn, Stanley thought, female flesh.

Stanley let himself into the hallway of his lodgings, planning to retire early with a library book about great men of the Industrial Revolution. He liked that kind of thing. Railways; canals; bridges; mills; tunnels; engines. He was looking forward to an outing on Sunday to see a beam engine at Brighton, made before Waterloo and still working, though now tended as a hobby by solicitors and accountants who competed for the privilege of shovelling coal and raking out ashes. It was because Stanley knew that much of the English industrial landscape had been hewed by Irish navvies that he had gone to the lecture. Stanley knew that the word navvy was derived from *canal navigator*. He had a drawerful of notes that he dreamed of turning into a book illustrated by prints of early water closets, sewing machines, gas works. He would make himself a nice cup of cocoa and read his library book in bed. There was a chapter about the great Brunels, father and son. Isambard Kingdom Brunel was Stanley's hero. Reading about him was almost an act of worship. Stanley, timid, sedentary, bookish, venerated the archetypal man of action: genius; wheeler-dealer; fixer of parliamentary bills; tunneller; inventor; floater of companies; architect; maker of an age; undaunted by sickness; flamboyant to the end; his short, packed life as moving as that of Keats.

In the hallway he met his landlady's son. The youth had obviously just spent hours squeezing his pimples and arraying himself in all the splendours of a style called Edwardian: drain-pipe trousers; winkle-picker shoes; boot-lace tie; side-burns, and now, like Beau Brummel, he emerged *insolent from his toilet*. Youth, thought Stanley enviously, thoughtless youth, and then from some unaccountable whim translated it mentally into a Dublin accent. Yoot. Tawtless. A tawtless yoot. He nearly giggled. The youth looked at him in surprise and resentment. He was not accustomed to arousing amusement in Stanley, let alone what was to follow, for Stanley had experienced a sudden influx of boldness. It was something to do with the thought of Mr Trelford exacting tribute from his Irish vassals in the form of being pleasured by their women after hours in the I.K. Brunel building with the pretty cupola.

'Oh ah!' Stanley roared in authentic Trelford accents, conveying by that flexible all-purpose West Country exclamation mock amazement tinged with derision, 'well I be buggered my old beauty! Oh ah m'dear!'

It was not only the youth who was startled but his mother. Mrs Malloy poked her head round a door in surprise. She was a still good-looking bottle-blonde Dublin woman who could be rather formidable as she was the daughter of a publican and had learnt from both sides of the bar how to be tough with men. Indeed Stanley did not merely read her notices and obey them implicitly – like the one in his room saying *This gas ring is for beverages only* – but imagined them being spoken by her standing with her hand on her hip, and he marvelled at the bravery of some of the other lodgers, mostly Irish, having surreptitious fry-ups after what they called 'a feed of drink'. She had summed Stanley up as a quiet man who would give no trouble. She now blocked up the stairs with her hand on her hip and expertly smelled his breath to try to account for the carry-on in the hall, and while she was at it she decided to question him about something else it had not occurred to her at the time to be too suspicious about.

'Here,' she said, 'what were you doing in that woman's room the other evening?'

'Well,' said Stanley nervously, quite abandoned by the Trelford persona and left to face the consequences, 'I was fixing her gas fire.'

'Her gas fire is it!' Mrs Malloy said scathingly. 'Do you know what that woman is?'

'Well,' Stanley said uncertainly, 'I understand she does evening work.'

'Oh she does surely,' Mrs Malloy confirmed bitterly, 'that woman is a tart. Did you not know that?'

'No,' said Stanley in surprise.

'Well you're the only bloody one in the house that doesn't,' Mrs Malloy said, 'I'm going to get rid of her. What the hell were you doing to her gas fire?'

'A burner was blocked,' Stanley explained, a little more confident about technical matters, 'I was poking it.'

'She had two short times in this evening,' said Mrs Malloy grimly, 'and it wasn't her gas fire they were poking.'

Stanley's mouth fell open in a kind of awe. He was the son of a Ballymena Presbyterian minister and thought himself very emancipated to be living in a house full of Catholic Irish. Mrs Malloy stood aside to let him pass and watched with amusement as he tried to digest the fact that he was on speaking terms with a prostitute.

'I'm trying to catch her at it,' she called after him, and then added with a laugh, 'so don't you go poking her gas fire again.'

Her feelings of amusement softened her. He was, after all, a nice obliging man who gave no trouble, and if bantering at that eejit of a son of hers meant he could get his paddy up, what harm in it, God help his innocence. She had before then been sometimes moved by maternal feelings to heap up his plate with her good meat stews to put a bit of flesh on him. 'Stuff that into you,' she had urged. 'That'll put a bit of blood in you,' she had said.

But another feeling touched her now that was not entirely maternal. He wasn't a bad looking man when he got you to notice he was there. She patted her hair into shape at the mirror and made a mouth to check the state of her lipstick.

A little later Stanley was in his pyjamas; his book was on his bedside table ready to open at the tooled bookmark that had been a Sunday school prize for bible knowledge. His kettle was already boiled for his cocoa when there came a soft knocking at his door.

Doreen

When the young male bed-sitters heard that the first-floor vacant room had been let to a single woman they were hopeful that she might be young and pretty, even though the word used by the housekeeper had been 'youngish' rather than young. When they saw her they were a little nonplussed. Yes. Well. Bit past it. And such awful clothes. Her name was Doreen and she clearly wouldn't see thirty again. Very middle class and church-going. No. Nothing there, although she went out of her way to let them all know she was a lively person and a bit of a sport. 'Did they ever have parties in this house?' she enquired loudly and brightly. They did at the last house she was in which had been in Trebovir Road. She used the term Trebovir Road to refer to this last house. 'The Trebovir Road people', she would say 'had very wild parties.' Australians. She had a theory that Australian men were very, well, you know . . . She had all sorts of theories about the kind of people who were highly sexed. A quiet man on the third floor who came and went unobtrusively she referred to as a man who was very, well, you know . . . How did she know? 'His eyes,' she said, 'his bulging eyes. People with pop eyes are all like that; women,' she conceded, earnestly, 'as well as men.'

Doreen came to the party in the second-floor double in a dress that had the girls all laughing at her behind her back. She had made it herself specially for the party. It was long and trailing and bits hung from it. Moreover, it was rather thin, and when she turned swiftly so as to spread out the fullness of the hanging folds it was obvious that she had no underslip on. She told people loudly that she had got the idea for it from the Indian women's sari, and spun round for them to admire it, trailing one of the hanging bits in her hand. She launched into a loud discussion with two young women wearing crosses about the Anglican ritual and which churches in the neighbourhood were 'High', and also about the attitude of the Anglican and Roman Catholic Churches to divorce and birth control. It so happened that a lull in the music occurred just as Doreen said very loudly with an airy wave of her hand, 'Oh, I know all about the withdrawal method.' People laughed about that for a long time afterwards. They also laughed over the way she had made an exit from the party, carried over the threshold by the quiet man with the pop eyes, and languidly trailing a hand. She had dared him to. 'I double dare you,' she said, and the poor man had no option though he had clearly been worried about her weight without wanting to show it, for though not big she was quite sturdy. People long recalled the exaggerated way she had lain in his arms as if being borne off by a sheikh. 'Did they . . .?' people said to each other. 'No,' they scoffed. 'She's an old maid.'

One day Peter was in his room. He was taking the day off. He was not sick or anything but just felt it would make a change not to go to work. He sometimes did that when vague feelings of loneliness and dissatisfaction assailed him on waking. There was a knock at the door. It was Doreen. She was wearing something bright coloured, but odd. It was odd because she was in the process of making it and parts of it were gathered up with pins. She spun round in front of him with her arms outstretched and asked him eagerly if it would do for the next party. 'Well?' she smiled at him, and Peter said hastily it was very nice, while storing away in his mind as something with which to amuse people the picture of her stepping back and spinning round like a model at a fashion show. But something else struck him. As she spun round, the dress or skirt or creation or whatever it was had lifted very high to show her thighs and beyond. He had caught a glimpse not only of her knickers, but of the fact that they were of such a thin material that he was sure he had glimpsed something through them that was dark but not shadow. He felt strangely shy because of it. 'Come and have coffee,' she said cheerfully. 'Mind the pins,' she warned as she brushed past him at her door. While the kettle was boiling she put on a dressing gown so that she could take the pins out under it. Peter wondered what it all meant. He was not an expert in recognising invitations from girls and had missed many an opportunity in consequence. They can't mean . . . he had thought, and by the time he had plucked up the courage to see if they did mean . . . it was too late.

'No need to talk is there?' Doreen said encouragingly. 'When two people are in harmony there is simply no need to say a thing. I could feel the harmony when you answered the door,' she said. 'Wouldn't you be more comfortable on the bed?' and she made him lie on the bed after they had drunk their coffee. She sat on the edge of it and spoke wearily of her mother in Surrey with whom she was always having differences of opinion about religion. Her mother was not 'High' and was quite strongly opposed to the Catholic religion which Doreen was attracted to. She said she would have to go and see her on Sunday. No doubt her sister would be there with more lurid tales of her beast of a husband. 'He's got these slightly protruding eyes,' said Doreen. 'Never leaves her alone,' Doreen confided to Peter. 'Every night. Even when they're at mother's. He's got these pop eyes.' Peter said, 'Really?' and Doreen nodded very seriously. 'He makes her, well, you know . . . '

'What?' said Peter, also made serious by her earnestness.

'Oh, you know,' said Doreen, '*Do things*.'

'Oh,' said Peter.

'Yes,' explained Doreen, 'even when she was pregnant he had to have . . . And he can be quite well, you know.'

'What?' said Peter, in awe.

'Well, violent, almost.'

'You mean he hurts her,' said Peter.

'Good heavens, no you silly boy,' said Doreen brightly,

'not *that* kind of violence, but, well, you know, rapes her, almost. I heard them at it,' she said with a sigh.

'Did you?' said Peter, shocked.

'Yes,' said Doreen, 'at mother's. I was sleeping downstairs on the settee. They were in the bedroom above. I heard this sound. I thought, it *can't* be. But it was.'

'What?' said Peter.

'The bed,' said Doreen. 'But so *fast*. And it kept on and on, and got *faster*. Oh no, I thought, you brute, I thought. I asked her straight the next morning. "Did that brute hurt you?" I said, but she said, "only a bit." I was going to speak to him about it but she implored me not to. It seems,' said Doreen with a sigh, 'that that would only make them worse.' Doreen slipped into the *general* case sometimes and spoke of *they* and *them*.

'Anyway,' said Doreen, 'they sometimes well, you know.'

'They?' said Peter, wonderingly.

'People like my sister,' said Doreen.

'What?' said Peter.

'Oh, well, you know, a bit of a masochist. I sometimes think she likes being half-raped. Some women do, you know.'

'Do they?' said Peter, his heart beginning to beat violently.

'Oh yes,' said Doreen confidently, waving her hand airily rather in the same way that she had waved it the time she had said loudly that she knew all about the withdrawal method.

How should he start? He cleared his throat nervously. 'Your dress looked nice,' he said.

'May I lie down beside you?' she said brightly, and they lay side by side without touching or talking.

'I know,' said Doreen eagerly, as if an idea had struck her.

'What?' said Peter, realising that time was slipping by.

'Why don't you come to St Ethelred's with me on Sunday. It's not *all that* high,' she said knowledgeably, as if that might have been stopping him.

'Yes,' said Peter, relieved that he would get another chance. After church. On Sunday. He really would. He would pinion her arms by the wrists to the corner of the bed in the most brutal fashion and plunge into her violently, going faster and faster and faster, so that she could confide to her sister how he had well, you know . . .

Violence

The voices of the workmen digging the hole in the pavement could be heard in the nearby houses. The workmen cursed a lot, or rather they employed with monotonous frequency one particular four-letter word even when they were talking quite casually. Mr Croker's house was not the one nearest the hole but he found his attention being increasingly caught by the sound of the four-letter word. It made him very uneasy. He began listening for it, standing quite still with his head cocked. When it was spoken particularly loudly he felt a little stab of dismay in his stomach. What made him uneasy and dismayed was the thought of what he ought to do. He really ought to go out and speak to the workmen and ask them to moderate their language. It was not good enough for him merely to go to the window and move the curtains about to let them know that he was there, or even to open the door noisily and scrape his feet. Even when he stood at the window or the door and stared straight at them they merely glanced at him indifferently and went on using the four-letter word as freely as before.

Mr Croker continued to feel upset long after the workmen had packed up and left. He could not put them out of his mind. No matter what he was doing there would come into his mind an imaginary scene of confrontation between himself and the men in the hole. And in this scene, no matter what his manner in addressing them; man to man; denunciatory; reasonable; sarcastic, it would always end the same way.

The men would exchange brutal leering looks and tell him contemptuously to fuck off. 'Ah, fuck off,' they jeered.

Their contempt lay upon his mind like a dull ache. It asserted itself as he cooked himself his meal and rendered it tasteless. When the television news showed its usual scenes of violence and cruelty, or faces blandly smoothing over injustice which would normally have filled him with the urge to beat at somebody with his fists, there came between him and the images on the screen more urgent pictures of himself at bay before the jeering workmen, reduced to impotently yelling at them in fear.

When he read his bedtime book, a habit that was normally such a consolation to him, he found his imagination still seeking, endlessly seeking, fresh scenes of confrontation in which the contempt directed at him could be undermined. There came a point where, much against his better judgment which continued – though unsuccessfully – to resist his dwelling upon what gave him so much pain, he flung aside the bedclothes and went to the window. There he stood, staring down for a long time at the silent empty hole marked by red lamps where he had suffered such a humiliating defeat.

The Gesture

Mr Campbell hated anti-Semitism, colour prejudice, all forms of bullying. But privately. His feelings when he encountered them were of dismay rather than anger. Indeed he was somewhat inclined to laugh weakly when jokes or accusations against Jews or coloured people were made in his presence and then reproached himself afterwards for not having the strength of character to speak out against it. If he could even have been coldly silent. If he had done no more than frown disapprovingly. But he dreaded being the object of attention, being the odd man out.

Even with regard to ordinary straightforward bullying he was always finding himself in a false position. What on earth did you do when a man who was very civil to you, and indeed whose civility to you in a new job among strange people made you feel grateful, suddenly began picking on a harmless young fellow and holding him up to ridicule for no other reason than that the young man wore a little gold cross and had deep religious convictions?

Mr Campbell was presented with this problem in the staff canteen not long after changing his job. Staff canteens can be tricky places for newcomers who do not make friends easily or take new acquaintances in their stride. People like Mr Campbell learn to be very wary of going into staff canteens on their first day and sitting in a seemingly empty place because a lot of the places turn out to be ones that groups use regularly. Oh they may be quite nice about it when they find someone like Mr Campbell sitting in one of their seats. 'No, no, old chap,' they say, walking away with their arms full of plates and cutlery, 'hasn't got my name on it you know!' But it is perfectly obvious from the restrained way in which the others converse around that table that their lunchtime routine has been disrupted. So it is necessary, but not always easy, to find a table where just *anybody* sits. That was why Mr Campbell felt rather grateful to the man who, during his second week, came over and sat beside him and engaged him in conversation. It turned out that he was new too. After a little while those places became *theirs*. Then the man brought along another, younger man from his department, the one who wore the little gold cross, and also a little badge on his tie. Mr Campbell could not make out what the motif on the badge was but he felt sure it was another testament to his Christian beliefs.

Suddenly one lunchtime the older man began taunting the younger one about his piety. What made Mr Campbell especially unhappy was that the man kept turning to Mr Campbell for corroboration. Then the baiting took a coarser turn and the man wondered leeringly how the young Christian could keep his wife 'satisfied' if he was such a holy Joe.

'He'll find out,' he said to Mr Campbell grimly, 'he'll find out, won't he. You don't keep them satisfied, somebody else will. Eh, Mr Campbell?'

And Mr Campbell laughed weakly, even though he was a single man, very shy with women, and all that side of life was beyond his experience.

Mr Campbell's inability to stand up for his principles worried him. He often brooded upon it. He would mentally re-enact the young Christian being taunted, seeking a version in which he was able to be the kind of person he thought he should be. Too often, however, in these mental re-enactments he would be unable to avoid shouting and getting red-faced, with people turning round to stare.

Then there was a sudden death in his department and a collection was taken for a wreath. From the remarks that were passed Mr Campbell gathered that the man was Jewish. The notion came to Mr Campbell that he should attend the funeral. He got quite excited at the idea. He felt that it would somehow make up for his cowardice in laughing weakly at anti-Semitic jokes. The thought of having decided to attend the Jewish funeral made him feel better, even when he sat silent as the man at lunch continued mocking brutally his young Christian colleague.

He had great difficulty in finding the cemetery in the East End. He had to ask his way and was relieved that the woman he stopped did not give vent to anti-Semitic remarks in the course of directing him. When he reached the cemetery there seemed to be nobody about. Then he noticed a building from which came the sound of people talking, but in unison like chanting. He went in, and it was indeed the funeral service. The room was filled with people. A robed minister was singing something holy in a strange language. All the women were standing down one side of the room, the men down the other. Mr Campbell found himself the object of embarrassing attention. A book was put into his hands from which the people spoke in unison in between the minister's singing. The pages had Hebrew down one side, English down the other, but he could make nothing of it even though some of the people were chanting in English. The man at his side indicated with sign language that the book read from back to front. Mr Campbell saw with surprise that the last page was numbered one.

His consciousness of being different and conspicuous was acutely heightened when he noticed that all the men except himself were wearing something on their heads. With some it was a little round skull cap but others were wearing ordinary hats and wearing them, it seemed to Mr Campbell, in a surprisingly casual manner, jaunty almost, tilted racily to one side, or even pushed to the backs of their heads.

The Rabbi, who had glanced several times at Mr Campbell, suddenly broke off the service and came over to him. He was a tall, powerfully-built young man, not in the least the kind of figure Mr Campbell had been expecting: stooping, bearded, patient, inured to centuries of insult.

'Would you please cover your head,' said the young Rabbi coldly.

Mr Campbell, shamed and flustered as he was, nevertheless at that moment recalled with perfect clarity something he'd once heard said about Jews which he'd paid no attention to at the time: that Jews are the very opposite to Christians in regard to the covering of heads in holy places; it is women who bare the head, men must not. He was committing a profanity. What was he to do? What would be least embarrassing? It was so far to the door, which was on the women's side. Even in his distress Mr Campbell wondered at the segregation of the sexes, women down one side, men down the other. His wonder was tinged with anger, for it meant that he would have to run a kind of gauntlet if he simply walked out. Panic seized him at the thought of having to pass humiliated between those two groups like a corridor of shame. His hand closed over his handkerchief and in desperation he wondered if that would do to cover his head with. Knotted at the corners perhaps. His mind in a turmoil tried to wrestle with the problem of whether holding up the service while he tied knots in the corner of his handkerchief like an old fashioned day-tripper at the seaside would be less dreadful than having to leave.

'I never wear a hat,' he said desperately to the Rabbi who was looking at him not merely with disapproval but hostility, and showing not the slightest sign that he appreciated that Mr Campbell's presence was a gesture of solidarity with the persecuted and the oppressed.

'I must ask you to cover your head,' said the Rabbi brusquely.

Mr Campbell felt something being pushed into his hand. It was a brightly coloured headscarf. One of the women in the congregation had passed it across to the men to pass along to him. Desperately he draped it round his head and would have tied it under his chin if a sudden wave of rebellion had not stopped him. He looked foolish enough. He would do no more. He wished he had had the courage to leave. The Rabbi resumed the ritual.

Dumbly Mr Campbell waited for an end to the service and to his misery. When the time came he pushed the scarf into the hand of the man standing next to him and hurried out of the synagogue. He watched from a distance the coffin being carried along a path among the tombstones. No solemn procession. No pall bearers with measured steps. A crowd of people walking just anyhow and the coffin carried clumsily among them, the women wailing noisily but the men with their hats still perched jauntily on the backs of their heads, some with their coats hanging open and their hands in their pockets.

He had never felt himself to be such an outsider as now. All the other times from childhood onward when Mr Campbell had been an outsider came suddenly flooding into his mind.

Mr Campbell took a long time to recover such small self-esteem as he possessed. Gradually the episode faded from his mind. The only part that retained its sharpness was something that had meant little at the time: the faint perfume on the woman's scarf as it lay lightly brushing his burning face.

The Salt Cellar

It started innocently enough, as these things do. He broke his salt cellar. He thought it would be a simple matter to buy another. But they wanted him to buy a set, both salt and pepper. He was opposed to this on principle. He was very strong on principles, or rather he thought that he ought to be. He forced himself to adhere to the doctrine that it was the principle that mattered. Whenever he bought things he would hope and pray that there was nothing wrong with them because if there were he would make himself take them back. He rehearsed what he would say; he would imagine the indifference or even hostility that he would have to overcome; he would marshal his most telling arguments, he would hesitate outside the shop with a wildly beating heart and then rush in shouting passionately. On this occasion being told that he would have to buy a pepper pot he did not need made him quite passionate. The shop assistants were sympathetic. They could see his point. But they couldn't break up a set. Had he tried the hardware shop in Kensington High Street? The man in the hardware shop asked him loftily what he meant by a salt *cellar*. Did he mean a salt *shaker*? He did not wish to seem pedantic, he continued with the tired air of a man being patient with ignorance, but a *cellar* was a jar and we do not sell salt shakers on their own. He was caught off-guard. It always flustered him when officials and shop assistants said things he did not expect. 'Oh, for God's sake,' he burst out wildly, made unsure of himself by the calm assurance with which the man had pontificated.

He found himself on the street flushed and dissatisfied. All his life he had called it a salt *cellar*. He felt almost sure that everybody else did. How dare that man patronise him? He was *nearly* certain it was a *cellar*, not a shaker. He hung about on the pavement being *almost* positive enough to rush back in and challenge the man but not quite. He had better be 100 per cent. He would have loved to accost the passers-by. What a triumph *that* would be. He imagined a few passers-by quietly hearing him out, the discomfiture of the supercilious shop man and his own complete vindication. He noticed a Lyon's tea shop nearby. Of course. They would have them on all the tables. People would be using them. He went in and bought a cup of tea. He sat down at a table where a man was eating. How to get him to say salt cellar?

'What,' he asked in a voice he tried to make as off-hand as his excitement would allow, 'what do you call this?'

The man looked at him suspiciously but said nothing.

'No, seriously,' he appealed, 'what do you call it?'

'The salt,' the man said grudgingly.

'The salt *what*?' he demanded, unable to conceal his impatience, but realising that he too called it 'the salt' as in 'pass the salt', and adding, 'I mean the name of it.'

'Piss off,' said the man threateningly.

He found himself outside, almost sick with dismay. To be taken for a nutcase on top of being made to look small. Oh dear, oh dear. What a disastrous Saturday morning. No wonder they said that spilling salt brought bad luck. Dumb with misery he went back to one of the shops that sold the sets and bought one. The set was fixed to a card on which there was a printed blurb extolling their special virtues. Kept the salt and pepper dry. Special invention. Sole patent. He read it dully and without attention. He was so inattentive that he read without at first taking in the words 'salt cellar'. *Cellar!* So he had been right. 'I do not wish to be pedantic,' he heard again the supercilious tones and was filled not only with rage, but, for the first time, with resolution and self-assurance.

Trembling with excitement, he hurried, ran almost, back to the shop where the man gave himself airs, and as he ran he savoured the sweetness of the confrontation!

But the shop was closed. Saturday was half-day closing. He could have cried with frustration. Through the glass he could see the very spot on which the man had said snootily, 'I do not wish to be pedantic' . . . and on which by rights he should have been paid back.

He paced up and down the pavement, almost yielding to the impulse to explain the situation to passers-by.

He thought for a moment that he saw a fellow he knew slightly, going into the launderette near Lyon's. He longed to pour it all out to him, being bitterly ironic about the printed word *cellar* on the card. But when he looked in the launderette the man turned out to be a stranger.

His lunch was tasteless in his mouth as he brooded upon the events of the morning. He would have to take Monday off. There was nothing else for it. If he left it till the following Saturday the man could pretend to have no knowledge of the incident. Unless . . . unless he could somehow trap the man into repeating his arrogant display of ignorance. No, he could not rely upon himself to carry it off. No, it had to be done while the thing was fresh. Monday morning, first thing.

Gradually, he began to feel better about it. He began to see that it might even have been to the good that the shop was closed when he rushed round with the card in his hand. He might have spoilt his performance from being in a rage, put the man in the right by rushing at him shouting. He would not give him that satisfaction. He would be very cool. He would prepare himself.

That evening, as he stood at the edge of the dance floor in Kensington Town Hall watching the couples on the floor and later, as he sat alone in various public houses slowly sipping his drink, he felt comforted by the thought of striking back on Monday morning. He let his mind play alternately with anger over the words 'I do not wish to be pedantic', spoken as they had been, and with his own triumph over the refutation of those words by the description 'salt cellar' printed boldly on the card, his trump card. It warmed him more than the beer to think of the victory he would at last score over the world on Monday morning!

Rags

The big red plastic bag containing his wife's clothes sat on the landing for a long time. He planned vaguely to give them to some charity or for jumble. Once he put the bag on the back seat of the car and drove to a converted shop that advertised for clothes for famine relief. But the shop was shut. A notice in the window set out the hours it opened. The hours were short, and varied on different days. What a stupid way to do business, he thought angrily. If they had been open he would have told them what he thought of trading hours that made it difficult for people to help, especially as you had to block the traffic to stop.

So her clothes were still there weeks later. Once the bag slumped over and some things fell out. A little brown jersey as small as a child's was among them. His heart ached as he put it back. Tears ran down his face and he walked up and down the landing groaning, seeming to be looking in each door for somewhere to turn. He called out her name.

Then one day he heard a bell and a strange sing-song cry as a scrap lorry toured the neighbourhood. It stopped near his house and two men got out to go into one of the houses. He went up to the lorry and asked a youth who was sitting on a scrap armchair ringing a handbell if they took rags. 'Yeah,' he said.

He went back to his door and waited with the red bag. Why had he called them rags? he accused himself angrily. They were not rags. Her beautiful little jerseys and blouses.

Her dear gaily-coloured little trousers. Why had he said rags?

Why were they making him wait at the door? When the youth eventually approached, he decided to be severe. 'I want the plastic bag back,' he said coldly, as the youth swung it up on his shoulder without bothering to look inside. He watched him clamber up the side of the lorry and toss the clothes, bag and all, on top of the junk beside the armchair. 'I said I want the bag back,' he shouted angrily and at that they reluctantly upended it. He saw all her garments tumble down among the old lawn-mowers, cookers and bent pipes. The youth sat down again in the armchair and emitted his weird cry and rang his bell. The red plastic bag was returned to him by one of the men.

What did he do now? Didn't they give money? Why should they get all her nice things for nothing? They weren't a charity. He would jolly well stand there making it clear that he was expecting payment. Why did they make him stand there waiting for money for her dear little clothes!

A big bald-headed man came towards him, lumbering and coarse-looking. The man thrust his hand deep into a trouser pocket with the slow deliberate action formed from the habit of throwing back the skirts of a coat or apron in a lifetime of sordid deals. He pulled out a handful of coins and picked among them. He selected two. Two shilling pieces. The scrap dealer's huge dirty paw proffered the two coins which dumbly he accepted and went back inside.

There he shook with rage and misery at the minute sum he had sold her clothes for and at his own spiritlessness in accepting it without protest.

That leering brute had insulted him and he had put up with it. In doing nothing about it he had fouled her memory. Could he not at least have said to him scornfully, '*You* don't give much, do you?' He put the two shillings among the rest of the change on his bedside table and after a while they were indistinguishable from the others.

But the picture of her little jerseys and bright little trousers falling down through the tangled junk, and of the brutal figure lumbering towards him picking over coins, haunted his mind and became a symbol to him of the hard-heartedness of the world.

As Good as a Teddy Bear

The morning after the party the big studio room was a shambles: empty bottles; full ashtrays; cigarette ends doused in half-filled glasses. People lay about all over the place. A row of people lay crosswise on a mattress that had been pulled off a divan bed and a trio lay neatly the right way on the divan base. Armchairs were filled to overflowing. Some people lay on the floor. Their stillness as the sun shone brilliantly in through the floor-to-ceiling windows was not so much due to sleepiness as to hangover lethargy.

For a long time no one moved. The first to bestir himself was a young man who felt so happy it made him want to get up. He was happy because he had fallen in love. A lovely nurse from St Mary Abbot's Hospital had danced with him in a very special way when they put on the trad jazz record by the Chris Barber band, 'Lawd But You've Been So Good to Me', and then had lain at his side all night. He could hardly believe it had happened, it was so wonderful. At the end of the party she had just come over and lain down beside him on some cushions on the floor, speaking hardly a word except to tell him briskly to get a blanket and in a daze of delight he set about obeying her. He tried asking couples to spare him a blanket but was angrily repulsed and when he tried just pulling the blankets off people he was threatened with violence. So he lifted an armful of coats off a trestle table and took them to where the lovely nurse awaited him. What happened later under the coats astonished him and in the morning he awoke so happy that he felt a great surge of benevolence towards all the people sprawled around him and he offered to make them all a hot drink of something if somebody would tell him where the kitchen was.

But then he saw with dismay that his wonderful lover looked up at him as if she did not know him, as if the night had not been. How could such a thing be? he wondered in bewilderment. Surely it was not possible to be a stranger to a girl who had helped him undo her bra and had drawn up her knees to let him slip her pants over her ankles? Yet there she was, cool and distant. In a little while she got up to go, stepping over the people on the floor, not even looking at him, leaving him not even her name. He thought wistfully of how happy he had been when she showed him how to bring the back of her bra round to the front to get the hooks out and how an enchanting vista had opened up before him of having a girlfriend, of having a girl at his side in the streets, in the coffee bars, in the public houses, on the grass in Kensington Gardens, a girl to be tender to, to buy silly presents for, to tease, to laugh with, to run his finger down her little nose, to cup her face in his hands. Why could it not have been?

Then he remembered. It was what she had whispered under the coats in the dark.

'Make me come,' she had whispered, 'make me come.'

She had whispered it passionately. Then pleadingly. Then impatiently. Then . . . was it angrily? Was it *contemptuously*?

So this Sunday was not, after all, going to be much different from other Sundays. Those London Sundays. Nowhere to go except parks, public houses, cinemas, museums, dance halls, political demonstrations. What was it to be? Bertrand Russell on the Bomb in Hyde Park? Brigitte Bardot at the Odeon? Carlyle's house in Chelsea? The Hammersmith Palais? The King's Head in Fulham? The Union of British Fascists' street meeting opposite Earls Court Station, where the speaker would get angry when he was heckled about the gas chambers and the Jews?

That evening in his own room he cried. He cried softly in case he should be overheard, and once, when footsteps approached his door, he stopped crying till they had passed by. He took something from the back of a deep drawer and looked at it for a long time. It was not a teddy bear, though such comforters are not unheard of among the solaces of grown men and have even been found in the effects of posthumously-decorated heroes. It was a little jar. It contained a substance he had seized eagerly and swiftly at a place of work. He had kept his fist tightly clenched till he could open it in secrecy and brush with excited gladness every grain into the little jar. It was potassium cyanide. There was a skull and crossbones on the container from which it came. Said to take only five seconds, though he had read somewhere that Himmler, the Gestapo chief, had needed ten.

He did not know how close he had ever come to using it, or whether he was closer on this occasion than on others. Perhaps he would never use it. Perhaps it was his teddy bear. Even when he put the jar away again it was still a comfort just to know that it was there.

Tomorrow and Tomorrow

Sunday afternoons he generally passed in the parks and museums. Sometimes he wandered into Hyde Park. There, rather than in the streets, he felt the vastness of London all around him. He would lie on the grass with a book from which he would raise his head to listen in awe to the roar of the city. Once, among the soap-box orators at Speakers' Corner, he heard a man denounce cities, describing them as 'pullulating excrescences', which drew a faint cheer from the grinning crowd that was egging him on. The man spoke contemptuously and with hatred, raising his arm to brand and denounce not only the streets and buildings that glinted in the distance but the sound, the great ring of sound that embraced them like iron.

'Oh, but surely not,' an elderly man protested in a cultured voice, 'surely cities are evidence of man's achievement.'

He never knew why the old man had defended cities. He hoped the old fellow was right. He wanted him to be right. He would lie on the grass with his book, listening to the great ring of sound, the muted roar, the unceasing hum, and, excited but timorous, feel its allure and its terrifying pitilessness. As the afternoon wore on into evening there would come upon him the apprehension that Monday was looming, filling him with a vague dread.

'But we have a woman,' the boulevards roared back, 'but we have a woman.' He had read that in one of his library books. Paris. A man alone. Yes, he thought, the great ring of sound is saying that too, all the time saying, and he thought with longing of the woman who had (she had, had she not?) waved and smiled at him.

A plump pretty woman with brown hair that might have been dyed, whom he had often admired furtively as she stood drinking with a group of sporty-looking men in the Bodega in Kensington High Street, astonished him once by giving him a quick friendly wave of recognition as he came out of the launderette with his week's washing. How, he wondered, could he possibly get to know her? When he looked at the bed-sit girls in the coffee bars and the ban-the-bomb marches it was her he thought of, notwithstanding her hair being dyed and that she was no longer young. But when he went to the Bodega she was not always there, or, when she was, she was part of the merry group. Although she would give him a little quick smile and nod – which he would afterwards think and think about – it was not enough to induce him to screw up the courage to approach her. Long after she had stopped coming into the Bodega she would sometimes come into his head, especially on long Sunday afternoons when he walked in the parks or through the museums, her laughter, her wave to him, her bright smile, and he would be stirred again by a pang of excitement and regret.

And so the months went by and his life continued in an even routine. Week succeeded week and if each Sunday night he went to bed feeling a vague apprehension about Monday, well, that too was part of the regular pattern of his days. The woman in the cigarette kiosk learnt to reach for his weekly two ounces of tobacco before he asked for them every Friday when he came out of the Tube and would exchange a little smile but no words. There was the launderette on Saturday mornings. There were his half dozen eggs one week and a dozen the next. He never had to stop and think whether it was a dozen eggs week or a half dozen eggs week. There being seven days in a week, he had eggs over from his regular egg a day and what he did with those odd eggs might also have become routine but somehow never did. In the same way he always managed to introduce an element of variety into going to the library in Kensington High Street to change his library books, or into choosing which of the local public houses he would drink in. Sometimes he managed to bring together these three elements: his library books; his drinking; his odd eggs. He would think suddenly as he came out of the Tube from work that he would go to the library that evening even though he had not meant to go. Of course it was not that he had meant *not* to go. It was just that he had given it no thought whatsoever. It always gave him a little thrill of pleasure when the idea popped into his head like that. The unexpectedness of it made the evening ahead seem suddenly to hold something in store to look forward to. Then on his way back from the library there would come into his head pictures of the interiors of public houses. He would pass several without committing himself. Then he would think, why not? But which one was he in the mood for? Where he could sit quietly, letting the drink take effect and looking forward to reading his book at his gas fire? Or where he could listen to the loud talk of different groups, which, as he began to glow a little from the drink, he could half feel himself to be part of? Sometimes he would waver in his decision for quite a long time, retracing his steps back to public houses that he had passed, even hesitating at the doorways and changing his mind again at the last moment. He never liked to change his mind once he was actually inside; even if he saw immediately that it was not the right pub, should anybody look at him as he entered, he would feel obliged to stay. That was why it was worth spending a little effort on the right choice. Then, if the choice of pub was right and as well as that the book was right, so that he looked forward to a good read, he might suddenly feel a craving for something to eat, something savoury, and what is more savoury than bacon and egg? He would get the old pan going on his gas ring when he got back and if his head was a little heated with the drink, what of it? It seemed a bit of an adventure to be filling his bed-sitting room with the aroma of egg and bacon late at night! He would chortle to himself at the novelty of it and deliberately exaggerate a hint of unsteadiness in his legs, just as if there was somebody else in the room to laugh with him at his little pantomime. Of course, when he used his gas ring at night to fry bacon and eggs the gas meter used up the sixpences and shillings faster than he had allowed for. He always kept a supply of sixpences and shillings in an egg cup and it would have annoyed him to run out of them just as much as it would have annoyed him to run out of eggs or library books. He liked always to have things like that well laid out beforehand. He would see the eggs diminish one by one and be comforted by the fact that he would be in the shop again before they were down to less than one. He would grow uneasy if he were more than halfway through his library book without another one in reserve.

There was a little padlock on the gas meter which the old woman from the basement emptied from time to time. She came with a great bunch of keys for all the gas meters in all the rooms, each key with a label on it which was not always correct. She came also with two grumpy little pug dogs that were very short of breath and filled the room with snuffling and wheezing. She talked to them very cheerfully as she sorted the keys, showing them when the label was wrong, saying to them, 'That isn't the young man's key, is it now,' getting them to wheeze and snuffle their agreement that it was certainly not and showing them the right one triumphantly as if they had helped her to find it. One of the little pantomimes with which he indulged his whim that there was someone else there was to pretend to break open the gas meter and pocket the coins. He exaggerated the force that would have been required, miming a brutal action with a great iron bar which was, of course, the whole point of the joke, since the little lock was so small it could almost have been wrenched open with the fingers.

However, notwithstanding his strict devotion to his little habits, he began to take days off work without good reason. He did it entirely on impulse as he lay half-awake in the few minutes after the alarm went off. He set the alarm purposely to have those few minutes of drowsy snuggling. They were his most sensual moments and he always had to fight a little battle against the temptation to extend them. This little struggle was always most severe on Monday mornings and there came a time when the thought entered his head just to lie in. He began to yield to the temptation more and more frequently and the temptation began to come to him earlier than when he woke. It would come as he went to bed on Sunday night. Then after a while it came on the Friday as he journeyed from work in the Tube and it made him so full of gladness that the woman who had his week's tobacco ready for him as he approached the kiosk spoke her first words to him. 'You must have had good news,' she said to him with a smile.

There came a time when he took the next day off as well and then, dreading the ordeal of having to give more and more excuses, the day after that. Each time he made the decision it was such a sweet feeling of relief that he felt a great surge of benevolence towards his fellow men which expressed itself in an unusually strong feeling of kinship with any loudly laughing drinking school he would be sitting within range of in the public houses.

One evening as his egg and bacon sizzled appetisingly the gas went out. There were no coins in the egg cup. Nor would there be any more until he had sold some more of his possessions. He had got quite used to selling things for a fraction of what they had cost but for sufficient to defer for long long days ahead whatever he would have to do then. He was annoyed with himself for letting his sixpences and shillings run out. It was such a disruption of the even tenor of his days that rage and grief filled him for a moment or two. He wrenched at the little padlock and it snapped without much resistance. The drawer was full of coins. First there was alarm at what he had done and then relief that it had yielded so much that he would not have to think about what to do next for days and days. He exchanged a rueful look with an invisible companion as he arranged the coins into neat piles. 'So we have come to this,' he said with an exaggerated groan, 'busting open gas meters.' The picture came into his head of some famous actor speaking these words on a stage in a deep theatrical groan of despair, and it was so funny that he nearly spilt his egg and bacon on the carpet from laughing so heartily. 'Tomorrow and tomorrow and tomorrow,' he declaimed, happy in the knowledge that he had at least a week left of days like the one he had just passed.

Lily of Laguna

When Mrs McQueen's bad foot worsened and it was arranged for her to go into hospital there was a party in her second-floor double bed-sitting room to see her off. Her friend Herbie from Belfast and Jock the Glasgow man from the first-floor back single sang and did turns. They sang duets and fluttered little pork-pie hats just like professional artistes

> Dreaming when it's raining
> Dreaming when it's fine
> Underneath the arches
> I dream my dreams away.

Mrs McQueen sat up in bed drinking gin and orange and wagged her finger at her foot for being obstreperous. What a pity her son from Manchester couldn't come to the party she said. She often spoke proudly of her son in Manchester who was a university lecturer, married, but, as she explained ruefully, with a bit of an eye for the girls – for which his wife, said Mrs McQueen, sometimes gave him what for!

'Eee by gum, she gives him gypo sometimes!' said Mrs McQueen admiringly. 'Didn't take after his father,' she said with a wry smile. She said that her husband had been a very strict man. One of the old-fashioned sort. Very respectable and church-going. Her son and her had had to watch their Ps and Qs when *he* was about! she said with a mixture of pride and awe. He had been very hard on their son, making him do everything properly, speak properly, say please and thank you properly, not get up to mischief like other boys. She and her son had sometimes been in trouble because of the things they did behind her husband's back. And she laughed fondly at the memory of it.

'Eee there was reet to-do,' said Mrs McQueen, lapsing into a very broad north country accent. She often did this. It was in order to show London people, who might not know the difference, that her own usual northern accent was in fact quite middle class. She loved reading. Stendhal was her favourite author. She said she must not forget to take *Scarlet and Black* with her into hospital.

The little incense sticks burning in saucers gave off an aromatic smoke which Herbie and Jock waved away with the artiste's pork-pie hats when it drifted in their direction, complaining that people might think they were poufs. Mrs McQueen explained candidly that the joss sticks were to drown the sick-room smell that she had tried to get rid of with air fresheners. She knew all about sick-room smells, she said, from nursing her husband. Such a jealous man, she said. Even on his deathbed. If he heard her paying the coalman even! Would they believe what he had said to her towards the end?

'He said, "Elsie," he said, "you can get on your back for them anytime now." What a thing to say!' She added understandingly that he was a greengrocer.

She looked on indulgently when Herbie and Jock, who had discovered a common bond in the Protestant religion and a hatred of popery, began singing lustily those old back-street Orange Protestant songs that are never sung in respectable circles. 'Dolly's Brae'. 'The Sash My Father Wore'. People had to clear a path to allow Herbie and Jock to march up and down between the dresser and the bed, Jock emitting the sound of bagpipes, raucous but tuneful, squeezing an imaginary windbag with his elbow, Herbie miming a flute in between verses of song:

> And if that doesn't do we'll cut them in two
> We'll give them a taste of the Orange and Blue.

Mr Galynski, the middle-aged landlord and a devout

Catholic, was trying in a corner of the room, rather shyly, wistfully almost, to chat up the shapely blonde nurse from the basement single and Mrs McQueen said with amusement that his wife wouldn't half give him what for if he got anywhere with that one. She waved occasionally to Herbie as if he was some way off, and little-boy like, had to be reassured from time to time that he was still the centre of attention. Twice he called back at her, 'A wave of,' which puzzled people till she told them what it meant.

'Wave. Of,' she explained, 'a bit of foolishness between Herbie and me. A wave of affection. You know. A feeling coming over you.'

'A wave of,' she called back at him fondly to let him know that she had heard him above the chatter and the singing as he and Jock put on the pork-pie hats again to sing 'Lily of Laguna'. She shook some talcum powder down her chest, just in case, she explained, she ponged in the heat and said that she never could take to the novels of Jane Austen. No blooming meat on them, she complained. She said that she did like things with a bit of meat on them, Eee, that she did.

Herbie fluttered his pork-pie hat just like an artiste and sang at the bed as if it were the Royal Box of a great theatre.

She's no girl for sitting down to dream
She's the only Queen Laguna knows
She is my Lily of Laguna
My Lily and my Rose

Mrs McQueen's sore foot turned out to be leukaemia and her son was sent for. People went to visit her until the end. Her mane of fair hair was spread across her pillow and she was gasping for breath for which she tried to apologise.

'I need a new set of bellows,' she gasped with a rueful smile.

Herbie stayed behind after her son left. He was holding her hand.

When she died her son stayed in his mother's bed-sitting room to make the funeral arrangements. Herbie moved into a single. Two of the other bed-sitters knocked on the door of Mrs McQueen's room the night before she was buried to say that they would like to attend the funeral. Also to return one of her books. Stendhal. *The Charterhouse of Parma*. 'What,' she had said reproachfully, 'not read Stendhal? Eee by gum!' When her son answered the door he was only half-dressed. He did not ask them in but came out on to the landing to tell them about the funeral and they caught a glimpse inside of the blonde nurse from the basement single drawing the bed sheet up to cover her naked breast.

After the funeral the undertaker settled up with Mrs McQueen's son. Herbie sat in the corner looking suddenly old and oddly gentle. 'A more lasting memorial,' the tall thin undertaker suggested urbanely, leaving a glossy booklet, 'perhaps you would care to study our very competitive prices,' but Mrs McQueen's son said, 'Not just at the moment.'

Herbie had cried at the funeral but was calm again. It was he who had brought the news of her death from St Mary Abbot's Hospital. The third-floor double was having a party and the sound of music and feet filled the house. They were playing 'The Rock Island Line' when Herbie knocked at the door.

> Oh, The Rock Island Line is a mighty fine line
> The Rock Island Line is the road to ride
> I may be right I may be wrong
> But boy you're gonna miss me when I'm gone

People always stamped their feet harder when that number was played and joined in the vocal part as they danced. Mrs McQueen would have been at the party were it not for her bad foot. She would have taken a little gin and confidentially recommended it to girls with difficult periods. Herbie would have sat with an arm around her. When he knocked at the door the tears were streaming down his face.

'Elsie's dead,' he said. He was the only person who called her Elsie.

London's Brompton Cemetery is vast. Its vastness had not impressed itself the day of her funeral. Only one car followed the hearse on its swift journey, oh so swift. The tombstones flew past.

Where had they buried her? Where are you my dear, where are you? At last there was a place of new graves. But which was hers? It was hard to tell, wandering from mound to mound with his bunch of flowers. Raising the suspicions of the cemetery staff.

Oh yes, they said, people steal the flowers all right.

Why? To sell? No! To put on their own graves! they said. They meant the graves of their loved ones. You'd be surprised, they said, the people that steal flowers from graves to put on their own.

Did he know the grave number? He should find out the number.

Oh my love, my love, where are you. Lost in this great city of the dead. Oh my love I am lost for ever. Lost and alone. Alone and lost.

A Thoughtful Man

Mr Hamilton married late in life and there were no children. He was a bookish sedentary man with a passion for order and fair play. He was forever writing letters to the papers or the authorities or powerful private bodies on issues both great and small. Reports in the morning paper or on the radio news of injustices done to the weak or the unimportant made him set out for work very angry. The Sunday newspapers with a liberal turn, given to reporting such things in fuller detail, caused him to boil with rage all day. Little cards were always fluttering through his letterbox. 'The editor . . . regrets that not all letters can be published.' 'The manager acknowledges . . . will reply in due course.'

Mr Hamilton's wife was proud of her husband's letters and sometimes got him to write one on her behalf to a shop or a manufacturer if she could get no satisfaction herself. She called the kind of letter which Mr Hamilton wrote a 'snorter'. 'You send them one of your snorters,' she would exclaim angrily, her patience exhausted. He would read aloud to her the bits from his 'snorters' that particularly pleased him. 'Your record for incompetence in this matter is still impressive . . . ' ' . . . cannot decide if your tissue of irrelevant and incorrect facts is due to cunning or stupidity.'

It was not only the inhumanity or the blunderings of bureaucracy that aroused his wrath but also individuals who displayed a disregard for the civic virtue of considerateness to others. He rebuked people who shoved ahead in queues, even more so when it was others rather than himself who had been pushed ahead of. He protested when people smoked in non-smoking compartments, blocked thoroughfares, parked their cars where they shouldn't, let their dogs foul pavements. He often came home upset and fuming after an encounter with such selfish people. Sometimes he would be unable to purge it from his mind for days. On the whole he could acquit himself better by writing 'snorters'. Once he even received an impressive-looking envelope with an embossed coat of arms on it: 'Her Majesty's private secretary thanks you for your communication . . . '

One day he was travelling in a railway carriage when a man of about his own age got in and promptly put his feet up on the seat opposite. It was a thing that Mr Hamilton disliked intensely. It seemed to be on the increase lately; people were doing it more and more. Mr Hamilton could not therefore let it pass unchecked. He pointed out very firmly to the man that people would have to sit where his feet had been.

What happened next was so bewildering that, as is sometimes the case when a sudden shock occurs, Mr Hamilton's mind at first refused to register what his eyes saw and tried desperately to offer an alternative explanation; namely that the man, who was stocky and coarse-faced, had unaccountably produced a package and unwrapped it in Mr Hamilton's face to disclose a lump of meat or a bunch of sausages. It was in fact the man's fist and he was waving it right under Mr Hamilton's nose, so that Mr Hamilton could plainly see, enlarged by proximity, the little black hairs lying flat across his fingers above the knuckles and the blue dirt under the thumb nail. The fist seemed to steam with an assortment of odours, some of them unspeakable.

'Don't you try that fucking game with me, mate,' the man said menacingly, 'don't you fucking try that game with me.'

The rest of the people in the carriage stared but nobody spoke or moved.

Mr Hamilton was unusually quiet over supper that evening. When Mrs Hamilton went upstairs later to see why he had been gone so long from his armchair she found him lying naked in the bath in a pool of blood. He had cut his throat.

Getting Into Shape for a Come-Back

Frank Maguire, the Belfast writer once nominated by the *Sunday Times* as the most promising new novelist of the year for his first book *Black Vortex*, had spent the afternoon meeting old acquaintances in the BBC club near Portland Place. The visit had done him a power of good. Though no longer as young as when one influential critic had hailed him as Protestant Belfast's answer to Catholic Dublin's James Joyce, he nevertheless felt the promise of his talents to be still strong. Meeting some of his old drinking companions among the producers and writers had warmed him more than the drinks – indeed he had consumed far less than they had expected, so much had their fellowship alone exhilarated him and put him in good story-telling form. Not one but had greeted him with pleasure. 'Long time no see, Frank. What are you writing now? When are you going to give us another book?' He had hardly needed the drinks to make him sparkle and scintillate as he had in the old days when he was on a script-writing team of a successful radio show. Those who had the time had gathered round to hear his anecdotes and yarns. He had them in a roar over the reason why he was wearing a dinner jacket and white tennis slippers. Her father's clothes had fitted him but not his shoes. *Her* father? This classy female he had met at a party. Knightsbridge set. County. Rode to hounds. Took him to point-to-points. Helluva time while it lasted. But of course got no work done. Must get down to some serious writing again, for Chrissake.

Frank Maguire had been in America for a time and had picked up the habit, fashionable among certain writers, of casual blaspheming and cursing while speaking seriously of literature, in order to demonstrate that they were not cissies, that they had, as it were, as much goddamn hair on their chests as any other son-of-a-bitch. When his audience in the BBC club mentioned a writer they all used to know Maguire referred scornfully to all that goddamn telling-it-like-it-is Gertrude Stein horse shit that Hemingway had got them all at.

'Her father did a goddamned classy line in dinner jackets for Chrissake,' Frank conceded as some of them humorously fingered the texture of the material and made appreciative tasting noises. He told them about her Afghan hound and its daily rump steak which one day he ate. They thought the story of eating the Afghan hound's steak so good that they asked him why he didn't write it up as a story. 'Just like you told it,' they urged him reproachfully, 'why don't you write it just like you told it?' and with a serious expression on his face he agreed that he must get down to some serious work again.

He mentioned casually that in Belfast where he came from these tennis slippers were called 'gutties'. Children used to wear nothing else but 'gutties'. And did they know where the word 'gutties' came from? Local Belfast dialect, they suggested. No. It came from the old-fashioned Victorian word for rubber. Gutta Percha. Gutta Percha soled slippers. The abbreviation to 'gutties' had persisted for a long time in Belfast. Old-fashioned Victorian Belfast. Where you daren't cut your grass on a Sunday, for Chrissake. Six goddamned days shalt thou labour and do all thou hast to do, and the seventh thou shalt keep holy. He told them the one about the Belfast couple who papered the bedroom on a Sunday and thought they were safe with drawn curtains and the children sworn to secrecy. But the children had gone round the neighbourhood – no doubt in their gutties – saying, 'Me ma and me da's in the front bedroom but we're not allowed to tell what they're doing.'

'Seriously though,' said Frank, 'the origin of words is fascinating,' and he launched them all into an eager discussion of the surprising origin of some in common use, which those who had to get back to committees and programme meetings wished they had more time to stay for. There was the difference between American and English. Frank quoted H.L. Mencken to the effect that the English were traditionally unable to tell ephemeral American slang from the true American English that would have graced the writings of Thoreau or Emerson. Then there was the migration of ballads, for Chrissake. The Irish ballad, 'The Bard of Armagh', crossed the Atlantic and then went west with the covered wagons where it turned into – guess what – 'The Streets of Laredo'.

As I rode out in the streets of Laredo
As I rode out in Laredo one day
I met a young cowboy all wrapped in white linen
All wrapped in white linen and cold as the clay.

When they spoke of a contemporary poet, Frank said that his 'Electric Jesus' was the best thing he had ever done, and quoted one of its most difficult verses straight off, to the admiration of the Assistant Producer of the poetry programme in which the poet had read 'Electric Jesus'. Frank's ability to quote extensively impressed them all, and some of the others in the bar not in the group around Frank gathered nearer to listen. He quoted Baudelaire. Goddamned Ezra Pound. T.S. Eliot, for Chrissake.

We have lingered in the chambers of the sea
By sea-girls wreathed with sea-weed red and brown
Till human voices wake us and we drown . . .

Yes, the afternoon in the club had done him a power of good and he left filled with a resolve to get down to some serious writing again. He could already see the bright dust-jacket of the book that he felt was gestating within him. He turned over with satisfaction the phrases that would be employed by the blurb writers. Graduate of Queen's University, Belfast . . . gravedigger for Belfast Corporation . . . Canadian lumberjack . . . merchant seaman . . . dishwasher in

New York Jewish restaurant . . . winner of the MacHenry Prize for the Best First Novel of the Year . . . distillation of rich experience. He shivered in the cool autumn air of the late afternoon. The dinner jacket, though of excellent quality, was too fine for warmth and he had no overcoat.

The coolness of the outdoor air speeded up the wearing off of the euphoria induced by the flattering company and the drinks. He remembered that he had not in fact met any of the men who really mattered when it came to getting the work on scripts that he needed to stake him for the writing of his next novel. It was true that people had promised to tell them he had called and he had left one or two phone numbers where messages would reach him: the Sloane Street flat of this classy bird he had been shacked up with; the bed-sitting room of the two young men in Earls Court where he was working on ideas for scripts.

He was not in the mood for returning to Earls Court, to the table littered with books – some of them from Kensington Reference Library with notices in them threatening to prosecute anyone who removed them – the mugs with puddles of old tea in the bottoms on which a white film had formed, the remains of a loaf on a plate, the acolyte eagerness with which Nigel and Ron did the hack work of looking up things, making notes, typing.

It was nearly opening time for the public houses and he thought of the Fox in Knightsbridge. Someone had mentioned it at the BBC club. One of the programme producers whom Frank had hoped to meet, a really big man when it came to commissioning the kind of popular arts programmes that Frank had worked on and could do so well, was said to be going there this evening. Frank knew the Fox and thought he would go on there instead of returning to Earls Court. He ought to go. It was strictly business. Notwithstanding his resolution to cut down on all that sort of thing he really ought to go. Nigel and Ron would have to understand that. It was an essential part of the business of getting down to some serious writing again. If they had been with him at the BBC they would have seen that. He resented the fact that Nigel and Ron were no longer as dazzled as they once were when he had been greeted in bars by people who had a name in publishing, show business, the press, and said, 'Hi Frank, what are you writing now?' At one time, to the little group that had formed around him in Earls Court, being in his company when such an encounter occurred would have been recompense enough for putting him up, feeding him, clothing him even (if their clothes fitted). Of course he also had to read what he described elsewhere as their crappy manuscripts. Awful autobiographical crap. Nigel's wasn't too bad but Ron's was the real my-life-and-times-so-far manure. But now the novelty of rubbing up against real live figures in the London literary scene was beginning to wear off the young people. They wanted to keep him at it all day. Writing wasn't like that, for Chrissake. He had only pretended to be amused when he found out what this GMW was that they were always saying to each other. He had thought it was the General and Municipal Workers' Union, though he couldn't see how any of that set would be trade union. No, it stood for Get Maguire Writing again. It was what the group was called. The GMW. For Chrissake. Nigel even argued about a beer or two at lunchtime. It was as bad as having a goddamned wife.

Wife. That reminded him. He had big trouble in the wife department. That solicitor's letter from Belfast had shaken him. At first he had thought it was some sort of joke. They used to play jokes like that when they were first married round about the time *Black Vortex* came out. When he answered the phone a cold severe voice would say, 'This is your wife's solicitor speaking.' And vice versa. Ha. Ha. But this was for real. 'Application will be made to the courts for maintenance . . . unless . . . custody of the children . . . desertion . . . possible divorce proceedings . . . '

It was so unfair. All he needed was a bit of time to get down to some serious writing again, and he could smooth all that out. He would descend on Belfast again with loads of presents. He had loved doing that. Especially at Christmas. Extra cases and bags just to carry the presents. Pockets stuffed with goodies and presents. Hugs and kisses. Parties. Taxi trips everywhere to surprise old friends. Arrive on them laden with gifts and bottles. All he needed was time.

Resentment filled him as he sat on the bus to Earls Court which he had boarded before thoughts about the Fox in Knightsbridge began to tempt him. Of all the times to pull a trick like this. It must be her goddamned mother. A year ago, yes. Hell, yes. Even six months ago. But *now*? When he was getting into shape for a come-back? OK, so he wouldn't knock out the champs. But he *had* gone ten rounds with Hemingway with *Black Vortex* and he had a book inside him now that would make Hemingway take a count of eight, and might even, dare he say so, have Proust and Joyce worried on the ropes!

A picture rose in his mind of himself and Nigel that very morning in Earls Court. The hired typewriter clacking away, Nigel typing the outline of a script on the migration of ballads for singers and actors, Ron making sure that the words of 'Waley Waley', the old English ballad, were as he thought.

> Oh Martinmas wind when wilt thou blow
> And take the green leaf off the tree?
> Oh gentle death when wilt thou come?
> For of this life I am weary
> Oh Waley Waley for love is bonny
> A little while when it is new
> But when 'tis old it waxeth cold
> And fades and dies just like the morning dew.

While he himself supplied the words of the Irish version without any need to check them.

> 'Tis youthful folly that makes men marry
> And so my love I'll no longer stay
> What can't be cured sure must be endured sure
> And so I'll go to Amerikay
> My love she's handsome my love she's bonny
> She's like good whiskey when it is new
> But when it's old and growing cold
> It fades and dies like mountain dew.

He saw and heard himself, stern in horn-rimmed glasses, dictate to Nigel the words of the voice-over commentary as the singer was faded out: 'Note how the song has changed from a *woman*'s song, the lament of a seduced and abandoned woman, to a *man*'s song, a broth-of-a-boy's song, the song of a love-them-and-leave-them-Johnny, a drinking song. Which surely says something about the Irish?'

He felt bitter that such a scene of sober literary endeavour could not be transmitted to his wife in Belfast as a reproach for her solicitor's letter or that she could not have been made to hear what he had said to Nigel about all this drinking and jackassing around having to stop. Again he saw and heard himself, still stern in horn-rimmed glasses, solemnly charge Nigel with the duty of seeing that they got their stint of writing done every day before there was any drinking. Only way. That was how the champs worked. James Joyce never touched a drop before he got his stint in. Pissed every evening. Did Nigel know that? Fact. Virtually a lush. But got his stint in every day before he hit the bottle. If only his wife's goddamn mother could have seen him warming up for the session that morning.

After he got off the bus he hesitated at the corner of the street of bed-sit houses where Nigel and Ron lived. He did not have enough money left for the Fox, not if a really good drinking school got going with a fairly big round. The Fox was a small quiet public house tucked away among the mews houses and expensive flats of Knightsbridge. The landlord was a portly little man who affected a white jacket in which to dispense drinks and whose butler-like manner combining servility and hauteur went down very well with his Knightsbridge clientele who shopped in nearby Harrods in loud upper-class voices and went into the country at weekends. The last time Frank Maguire had nodded at him discreetly to put a round of drinks on the slate he had hesitated just long enough to convey the hint that he would like the bar debt settled and might have to embarrass by refusing, however distinguished the people Maguire was with or how appreciative of his company. But Frank did not relish the thought of another argument with Nigel and Ron like the one he had had before lunch to get them to stake him for the BBC drinking club. Inviting them to come with him to the Fox so that they could meet the big BBC producer as well as classy Knightsbridge people was no longer the trump card it would have been once. As well as that he was not sure he wanted Ron along. Nigel hit it off with the Knightsbridge crowd all right, being almost public school himself, but Ron . . . that bum has to argue with them about voting Labour, for Chrissake . . . could have pushed that brown stout horse piss he drinks down his goddamned throat for arguing with that General about getting his teeth on the National Health.

After weighing these matters on the street corner in the cool wind he finally convinced himself that the landlord of the Fox would be good for just one more time, especially if he heard him talk business with the big BBC man. His spirits rose as he walked towards the Brompton Road, resolving to proceed to Knightsbridge on foot to save the fare.

A pleasant half-guilty, half-exultant feeling came over him, similar to the way he used to feel when he was first married and was making a clever escape from the surveillance of his wife for a night out on the town with the boys, especially the time of *Black Vortex*'s publication and she had come over to London when he had been doing all the book-signing publicity sessions in W.H. Smith bookshops. Sometimes he thought that their marriage had been as much part of the publicity campaign as the book-autographing in the shops. The press had loved them getting married. Local-lad-makes-the-big-time-marries-childhood-sweetheart. Children posted near the phone box in Belfast when he rang her from London. That was the guilty part of the feeling. But the exultant part was the thought of the bar-room and the talk, the *man*'s talk, that was in store for him.

Frank Maguire loved good bar-room talk more than anything else in life. *Good* talk, mind you. Talk that ranged lightly and widely over every damned thing under the sun, but with wit and knowledge. Literature. Good jokes. History. Gossip. Yarns. When he wrote *Black Vortex* he had always kept in mind a bar-room of interesting and well-informed people; people who had been around, done things, seen places, knew people. Of course they were not the people who bought the book and made it a hit. The people who bought the book were the other people you saw in bars, the shadowy people beyond the fringe of the drinking school, the people who edged closer, perhaps wistfully, to catch more of the stories, the wit, the good talk. The way some people at the BBC that afternoon, people he did not know, not in the group he was with, had moved nearer and nearer to where he was putting them all in a roar with his stories, had whetted his appetite and reminded him of how long it had been, of how starved he was of *that*, of how he craved it, of how little compensation women were. Frank Maguire still possessed an undiminished store of the man's man's contempt for men who couldn't get women. Goddamned wankers who had to buy their women or marry them. His getting on in years, his greying hair, the battering his face had suffered in bar-room brawls in New York, seemed to make women like him all the more. But good bar-room talk? No. That didn't happen as often now. Standing, glass in hand with people all round you, as had happened at the BBC club, while you put them in a roar or alternatively held them quiet to hear the story you were telling? It had been quite a while. Memories came into his mind of how good that could be. He remembered the great night out in Fleet Street after the broadcast of a show he had helped to script. The discussion about the difference between verse and poetry. Kipling. Ballads. Gospel Hall hymns. For Chrissake. He remembered the hush that had fallen on the whole bar, right the way along it, all those newspapermen, those hard cases, as he had recited verse to prove his argument. 'When the dawn comes up like thunder on the road to Mandalay.' And from '*Songs of a Sourdough*'. Robert W. Service.

> Now a bunch of the boys were whooping it up
> In the Mamalute saloon
> And the kid that handled the music box
> Was hitting a ragtime tune . . .

How he loved to whoop it up. No earthly joy was so sweet. But to do that you needed . . . what? Money. Yes, but not just money. Something else. Credentials of some kind. Wouldn't work if you were a nobody, however well you talked. You needed to have a bit of a name for something. Anything. Didn't have to be big, but had to be fresh, topical, not has-been. Just so that people didn't wonder, why is he a nobody if he talks so well? Wondering that made people uncomfortable and they might be inclined to edge away instead of edging nearer. He really would have to get down to some serious writing again, for Chrissake.

He quickened his steps along the Brompton Road towards the bright lights of Knightsbridge. He thrust his hands into the pockets of the classy female's father's goddamned classy dinner jacket and hunched his shoulders against the first chill winds of approaching winter.

The Emigrant

The ship carrying the young Belfast man Joe McCabe to Australia was in the Suez Canal when King Farouk was overthrown by General Neguib and other officers, one of whom was called Nasser. The ship's purser put out an announcement that passengers should not be alarmed but that nevertheless only those with full passports would be allowed ashore at Suez. Joe had a full British passport and not just an Australian Immigration Document. *His Majesty's Foreign Secretary Ernest Bevin . . . requests and requires . . . without let or hindrance.*

It was evening when they docked at Suez and only a few passengers went ashore. But Joe and an older man from the same twelve-berth cabin on H-deck ventured into the night streets of Suez. The older man had been in Egypt with the Eighth Army. It was very quiet, not like Port Said on the previous day. In Port Said boys in long shirts to their ankles had followed them through the crowded streets, tugging at their sleeves persistently with offers of their sisters for jig-jig, while more prosperous citizens in suits and fezzes astonished them by blowing their noses into their fingers and wiping their fingers on the walls. By contrast, in Suez the streets were nearly deserted. A man in a long dirty garment accosted them with a packet of naughty postcards which he would not let them see properly before purchasing. Another walked for a while beside them, speaking enticingly of belly-dancers, jig-jig places, and where there would be a woman and a donkey, but he seemed nervous and fled precipitately when there was a sudden clattering and grinding noise. It was a tank. The tank lurched out from a side street and stopped. The turret swivelled to point the gun straight at them and Joe was appalled. But the ex-Eighth Army man calmed him with reassuring words. 'Just having a look at us, old man.' He was an old Sidi-Barani hand, had been to Tunisia with Monty, up through Italy with the Eighth, veteran of Alamein, all that sort of thing. 'Don't wet your knickers, old chap. Driver can only see ahead, gunner taking a peek at us. Used to do that ourselves sometimes. Good Lord yes! Italy. Put the wind up the Eyetie girls when you looked at them like that. I'll say!' And indeed the tank did appear to lose interest, for, after seeming to squat down on its haunches like some grim iron beast it suddenly gathered itself together and sprang gratingly forward down another side street into the night. Joe said that they ought to go back, for God's sake, and his more nonchalant companion raised no objection, indeed walked as quickly as Joe back to the ship, sparkling with warm lights, glowing with safety.

Cosy in his bunk with a book down on H-deck, Joe raised only feeble objections when a young Dutchman who had only an Australian Immigration Document asked for the loan of his passport, claiming that he and Joe looked alike, 'Like same brodders, *ja*?', which was patently untrue. A little uneasy for a while, Joe soon forgot it as he lay half-reading, half-reflecting pleasurably on his recent adventure, composing phrases for the postcards that he would send off next day to Belfast, hinting at having witnessed the Egyptian Revolution first-hand in a few cool words that would perhaps encourage them to infer much more behind the admirable reticence. He fell asleep pondering the technical literary problem of how to *imply* having looked down the barrel of a cannon in a foreign *coup d'état* in a few nonchalant postcard words, very tight-lipped, very British.

He was awakened after midnight. A ship's officer in white shorts who was standing at his side said very politely but very firmly to please dress and come with him. *Please*. He must please do it. At once please. He escorted Joe up through all the decks to the gangway on C-deck where something was going on around the table at which sat the Egyptian police who checked passports. A little to one side was the young Dutch fellow looking very frightened. There were three black-skinned soldiers (Nubians? Joe wondered in fear) wearing tasselled fezzes and holding rifles in the at-ease position.

'Is this *your* passport?' an Egyptian at the table asked Joe politely, and, when Joe said yes, motioned him to stand with the Dutchman near the soldiers. Near? Or guarded by? Were they under arrest? Joe thought with horror of a stinking jail. He yearned suddenly for home – and his mother.

The Egyptians conversed softly for what seemed a very long time with an official in a different uniform from theirs, letting the young men stew in their fearful imaginings. Joe stewed for a shorter time than the Dutchman, for he noticed astutely that the other uniform was *British*. The British official's white shorts were immaculate, the socks folded over with absolute precision, the ginger hairs above the knee spick-and-span. *It was going to be all right*. Later – oh very much later – Joe would reflect complacently that he knew what it was like to be a citizen of an earlier empire in a distant province but still protected by the long arm of Rome . . . Caesar requests and requires . . . without let or hindrance.

'Don't ever do that again,' the British official rebuked them coldly in the clipped British way, and added with a straight cold stare, 'anywhere.' Oh especially *anywhere*. Where Pax Britannica did not hold or where the British Raj was no longer what once it had been.

Joe did not send his postcards from Suez, those cards in which he'd planned to be admirably reticent about having witnessed a revolution. He decided instead to send them from Aden, where, according to the purser's notices advertising trips and excursions in the ports of call, you could be taken by coach to see a camel train being loaded for a land voyage into Arabia, to the oases and walled cities of the desert. He would refer to that instead with a few well-chosen words. 'Like in the Bible,' he would say, already anticipating what he would see. That would go down better in Belfast. It would impress them more than being in at the overthrow of King Farouk, and – though he did not dwell on the thought – he would not be reminded of having thought of his mother when he was frightened. He was still too innocent to know that, like certain other secret guilts, it is not uncommon for a young man to miss his mother on such occasions, and sometimes even, in extremity, to cry out for her.

On his fourth day in Australia Joe saw a card saying 'Men Wanted for Mining Project' on the notice board of the Immigrant Hostel in Adelaide, South Australia. He changed trains twice to get there and each time the character of the train changed, as did the country it travelled through. When he was on the third train even the peeling gum trees gave out and there were only spiky bushes in the red soil. The train was small and primitive and the coaches had a little railed verandah at the back, just like in the cowboy films that had nourished the mental life of his childhood. Sometimes the train stopped for no apparent reason. Then it stopped where a man was waiting by the side of the track near Joe's coach. He saw the man carry a horse saddle to the guard's van and throw it in. They were in cowboy country.

After one of these stops a man came into the compartment and sat down beside Joe, whom he addressed with the alarming intimacy of the inebriated, speaking tipsily but with intense feeling about his most private affairs, or rather one affair in particular, that concerning his wife and a man whom the cowboy invariably referred to as a *bastard*. Joe had a little difficulty in following the Australian turns of speech, the half-cockney half-American accent, the purely Australian words such as 'crook' for sick, and the Australian usage of words like *presently*, which Joe, puzzled at first, realised had preserved the very different Shakespearian meaning of *immediately*, *right now*. The cowboy leaned his face into Joe's and told him that he did not blame *her* but *that bastard*. He seemed to assume that Joe had sufficient experience of life to know that a *bastard* can always get round a woman; Joe hoped that his features would not instantly betray the shameful secret that he was still a virgin and he tried to make the understanding noises of a man of the world. Joe listened at first uneasily, then with real alarm, to the cowboy's rambling but bitter story of his wife and *that bastard*. Only two things were to stay in Joe's mind. One was that the cowboy, at a certain point in the tale of trust betrayed, made a significant movement with his hands. It was when he was saying what he was going to do to the bastard when he caught up with the runaways. The movement was undoubtedly the loading of a gun. After the cowboy wandered off Joe screwed up the courage to mention it to a group of other men nearby, but they laughed, not unkindly, and sought to reassure him. How long had Joe been in Australia? Five days. They laughed, though in a nice way, almost envying his fresh innocence from Belfast and, blushingly, Joe retreated, unable to tell them the other thing that had alarmed him. It was when the cowboy said his wife had had a miscarriage and how crook she had been, oh my word she was crook, and they were not supposed to *do anything* for months and if that bastard *did anything* . . . at which point he made the movement which mimed the loading of a gun and Joe, blushing as he was for his innocence and his virginity, nevertheless did not believe that such a sordidly realistic detail could have been invented by a drunk to help put the wind up a greenhorn just off the boat.

At one of the stops, which was a real stopping place and not just where cowboys flagged the train down, there was a bar with little swing half-doors a bit like in the Westerns in the cinema, except that inside it was more like an English or an Irish pub. Joe was intimidated by the roar of talk that struck on the ear when he pushed through the swing-doors and he could not bring himself to elbow his way through the throng of loudly talking men, for fear that he might betray the fact that he was quite unused to ordering a drink anywhere, let alone in a swing-door bar full of roaring hard-cases in the middle of Australia. He wondered apprehensively what they would do with him at the mine.

At the mine the new arrivals were looked over by the chief

ganger, a giant with only one eye. His ferocious aspect concealed a kindly heart, for he assigned Joe, not to a work gang, high-earning and ever striving to earn more, where they would have half-killed him, but to duties of a lighter nature in the stores.

He quickly earned the approval of the chief storeman, a born-again Christian and ex-hard-case sheep shearer from Queensland who daily listened with imperturbable serenity to the curses and obscenities with which the miners requested gear and tools, almost seeming to take pleasure in it both as a reminder of his own sinful past and as a little cross to bear for his Saviour's sake. He would end the working day with the words, 'Well, Joe, another day's march nearer home' – meaning heaven.

The storeman asked Joe whether he knew a place in Northern Ireland called Ballymena and Joe had to try to explain why he laughed when he said yes, why people were amused when you said Ballymena, because Ballymena stood for all sorts of things that made people laugh like . . . well . . . if you knew anybody from there . . . and the storeman said he did. 'There was this fella in Queensland from Ballymena. Name of McCaughey. Big sheep man. Took forty shearers. My word. It was the time of the depression, jobs very scarce. But this McCaughey fella would always take on a Ballymena man. Well, one day this Chinaman turns up. "Sorry no work," he was told. "Ah you no understand," said the Chinaman, "you tell big boss fella me Ballymena man."'

'I'll tell them that one next time I write home,' Joe said.

'Son,' said the storeman, laying his hand on Joe's shoulder, 'I'd sooner you told them the one about being a *Jesus* man,' but Joe, being from Belfast, was too well-used to being proselytised by born-again Protestants not to be adroit in resisting it.

Even so, he sometimes stopped on his Sunday walks to listen surreptitiously to the storeman and a handful of believers singing a gospel hymn in the small non-denominational tin-roofed church to which priests and ministers sometimes flew in to take services. The storeman's band of the faithful sang with a lusty fervour that reminded Joe of the Gospel Halls of Belfast and, even though his belief had long since lapsed, touched his heart with the first pangs of homesickness.

> Through many dangers, toils and snares,
> I have already come;
> 'Tis grace that brought me safe thus far,
> And grace will see me home.

His Sunday walks took him well beyond the mining camp into the desolate bush. It was winter but still very warm. Once he encountered an enormous lizard from which he backed away in fear while it remained motionless, crouching. The peculiar red soil was streaked as if water had been poured over it and stirred. In the distance was a hill from which he believed he might see the horizon all around, as at sea. He tried to ask an aborigine whom he met to confirm this. The aborigine, or abo, as the men in the camp called the native Australians contemptuously, was dressed raggedly in clothes that did not fit him properly. Joe asked him about the hill, trying to explain why, which was that he missed the Belfast hills and longed for a change from the vast Australian flatness. But they did not understand each other, the one an exile from a distant land, the other an exile in his own land. Joe asked him about the lizard, or goanna, as it appeared to be called, and the aborigine said that it could run fast but that Joe could just about have caught it. Joe found it impossible to imagine himself running in swift pursuit of such a creature. A lapsed King Billy Protestant confronted a lapsed stone-age man and the gulf was too great for communication.

Joe might have walked to the hill and seen for himself, even though he was uneasy about being alone in the bush, as indeed were others on his behalf. The South Australian Mounted Police were uneasy and they did not hide their concern when their vehicle pulled up near him and they asked him where he thought he was going. They were called Mounted Police, Joe later discovered, from the days when they had ridden horses and even camels. Like the camel, their motor vehicle had an extra water tank in case of breakdown and this they let him know. They didn't think it was a good idea to go walkies in the middle of bloody Australia. Awful easy not to find a fella in the middle of bloody Australia. Too right. My word. There was that last fella they never found. Just a boot with a bone in it, my word. Hope the poor bastard had passed away peacefully before the goannas started on him, eh Bruce? Aw, too right. They addressed him as sonny and gave him a lift back to the camp which he did not like to refuse. He heard men say that when women arrived at the camp without good reason the Mounted Police invited them to leave in the same manner in which they had advised him against Sunday walks.

Joe soon mastered all the paperwork at the stores connected with the issue of materials and gear. He studied carefully the regulations of the Government of South Australia concerning the storage and issue of explosives and took it upon himself to enforce them more strictly. This might have caused annoyance and possibly worse had he not, somewhat unscrupulously, implied that the formidable one-eyed man was behind it, which enabled him to listen with a look of sympathy to complaints about all this effing form-filling, chitty signing, bastard counting. The last referred to a slate hanging on the outside of the huge sloping wall which enclosed the little pavilion in which the gelignite was stored. The purpose of the wall was to act like a gun barrel in the event of an explosion and project the consequences skywards; the purpose of the slate was to record the number of persons inside *at all times*. Joe insisted this included the case of a man stepping out to piss. Oh yes. Sorry. Have to tighten up. Foreman ganger. Yes *him*. Won't tell him what you said he could do with his slate and chalk, ha, ha.

Joe liked to handle the gelignite for two reasons. One was that it said on the boxes 'Nobel Pty Ltd Melbourne'. It gave him pleasure thus to contemplate the provenance of the world's most prestigious literary prize. The other reason was that handling the sticks of gelignite as nonchalantly as if they were sticks of seaside rock allowed him to move more confidently among the tough men and hard-cases. It even made him feel, albeit a little wistfully, that it might not be too preposterous to be thought a bit of a hard-case himself, even though his first beer was still to come and he had not yet obliterated the memory of his first and only attempt to order drink in a bar in Belfast when, nervously forgetful, he had asked for sherry, realising too late that it was – oh God – a woman's drink.

He had a two-berth tent all to himself on the street of tents outside the main hostel building to accommodate the expanding work-force. Each tent was equipped with electric lighting and a power point for appliances. One somewhat unusual appliance that Joe saw plugged in was a woman's hair curler. It was used by a Hungarian to keep the curl in his flowing moustaches which he cultivated devotedly; when people offered to light his cigarette for him he would courteously but firmly indicate with a warning hand that they were to take great care, and, as he was a huge and powerful man, they did.

Because of the Hungarian's Habsburg whiskers, Joe mentally re-christened him the 'Archduke Ferdinand' and wondered in awe what his life had been, he and the other foreigners: Czechs; Yugoslavs; Poles. The Australians referred to them as the DPs, after the Displaced Persons Camps in Germany and Austria into which they had been gathered, a human flotsam of war. They spoke German among themselves as their common lingua franca and always called Australia *Ostralie* even when they spoke English.

Joe had his first beer in the company of the DPs. He told them that he had now been three weeks in Ostralie and that he was from Belfast.

'And is it *belle*?' the Archduke Ferdinand asked him jovially.

Well, no, Joe admitted regretfully, no. He tried to qualify this with mention of the hills, the redeeming hills that saved his native city from being nondescript.

'Ah, the setting,' they said understandingly, 'like Napoli.'

'Well,' Joe said uneasily, trying to steer between truth and loyalty, wishing that he could be witty and lightly bantering but managing only to be earnest, as he explained that he did not actually come from Belfast itself but from a place near it, but if you said the place name people only asked where it was and you had to say Belfast, so it was easier . . .

'Oh I never do that,' the Archduke Ferdinand said severely. 'I am from Pesht,' he proclaimed, lifting his moustaches to clear the beer.

Pesht, it turned out, was on the other side of the Danube from Buda, its twin city. Budapest. Joe was chastened by this example of pride in locality that put the suburb before the famous city, and wished he had the strength of character to follow it or even to grow a moustache.

The Archduke Ferdinand produced a photo of a very pretty girl and showed it to Joe after giving it a smacking kiss accompanied by heartfelt groaning noise of a sexual nature. Joe asked him if she was a . . . a Hungarian. His hesitation let out that he had nearly said a DP which was derogatory.

'She is Ostralien,' the Archduke Ferdinand said, and then added slowly in Australian, 'fair dinkum, too right, my word.'

'You are a pommy bastard, ho, ho,' the Archduke Ferdinand told Joe good-humouredly, employing an Australian term for a certain class of immigrant that was at least as derogatory as DP.

Joe said that he was not, though making it clear that he was merely correcting a factual error and not bridling at a slight. No, it was just that he was Irish and therefore did not qualify. It was only the *English* that were pommy bastards, he courteously explained. He felt it was something they should know.

He was surprised at how pleased they were to learn this. It appeared to provide the explanation for something that had been puzzling them.

'*Nur Engländer*,' they told each other delightedly, 'pommy bastard *gilt nur für Engländer einwanderer*.'

One of them asked him why it was so. He tried to suggest things he had read about Australia which might account for this odd antagonistic feature in the relations between Australians and the people so close to them in kin that it was part of the Australian vocabulary to call England *Home*. Was it something to do with Botany Bay? The convicts? The squatters? The Eureka stockade? Gallipoli and Suvla Bay? But it was only the fact that interested the DPs and not the reason. In settling into their adopted land it was more important to be familiar with its curses and terms of abuse than with its history. Moreover history was not as interesting a subject to them as it was to Joe, who had not been caught up in it, had never been uprooted and tossed about in its storms. Joe was visited with a sudden insight to that effect, inspired by the drink, as was the benevolence. Filled with warm feelings and sympathetic understanding as he listened to them chattering in German, Joe nearly blurted out the question which, in sobriety would have been tactless and unwise: *which side had they been on*? It was the first time he had ever experienced the convivial effects of alcohol, the need to share its profound revelations. He suddenly knew why Australians called Englishmen poms, pommies, pommy bastards. Something to do with Waltzing Matilda and the vast Australian outdoors, the cult of maleness, the hard-case, drawling sun-tanned virility in the bushwacker hat, camping beside a billabong under the shade of a coolabah tree, waiting while the billie boiled, contemptuous of pale effete cousins back Home. This great truth was revealed to Joe as he listened to them mixing Australian words with their German, especially the Australian word for girl: *sheilah*.

'Aw, got this bloody sheilah in Dandenong,' Joe said ruefully in a very broad Australian accent, 'aw, ye know, too right, my word.'

They laughed. They took his meaning right away. The hard-case Aussie bloke apologising to his mates for having a girlfriend. Joe had an acute ear for the things people said and the social nuances behind them. Almost immediately after arriving in Adelaide he had detected in the snatches of conversation overheard in the streets the Australian male's ambivalence to the female, the Samson syndrome, the fear that she might sap and weaken the celebrated Australian virility. Aw, gotta see this bloody sheilah in Dandenong.

Joe supped his beer and repeated his imitation of the reluctant Australian swain. He would be called Bruce, he explained loudly, they're all called Bruce when they're not Kevin. The DPs egged him on. The Archduke Ferdinand wanted him to do it as a turn, up on the small stage with a piano and a microphone where enthusiastic amateurs in the performing arts sometimes attempted to entertain with mixed success: an Irishman whose own idea it was to sing 'Mammy' had not been applauded and indeed Joe had given his opinion that the only thing to do with the Irish Al Jolsons was shoot them.

'Why Dandenong?' they asked him curiously.

'Why not?' he asked.

'It is in Melbourne,' they told him.

'*In* it,' he repeated in a disappointed tone, 'not on the Murrimbidgee, the Darling River, Broken Hill, just a bloody suburb,' and they said 'Yes, why not?'

'Oh well,' he said vaguely.

His take-off of Brucie became more plaintive, more indignant at being snared, until it took on a note of repentance, recantation. A group of Australians playing cards at a nearby table began glancing over at Joe in displeasure, so it was perhaps as well that he had to leave hurriedly after his fifth beer. The Archduke Ferdinand helped him out, and said he would feel better in the air. The ground was behaving peculiarly. It seemed to be on hinges and swung towards him playfully from time to time. Once it came up and gave him a slap, but gently so as not to hurt him. It was almost enjoyable, till it began to whirl round and round despite his protests, and when it stopped he threw up.

He felt better after throwing up. Back in his tent he remembered some seasickness tablets his mother had made him take with him which he had never used and he searched his case for them to help dispel the nausea. An old envelope dropped out. He removed what was in it, a faded copy of a wartime magazine. *Picture Post.* August 28, 1943. He had kept it amongst his most secret possessions. It was the one that had pictures taken from German newspapers, illustrating what the Germans were being shown of the war. Heroic German soldiers on the Eastern Front repelling the attacking Bolshevik hordes. Goebbels touring a bombed German city, being cheered by its citizens, promising better air defences, hinting at a secret weapon. But that was not why he had kept the magazine, carefully hidden away in case his mother would find it and know why. It was the nudes. Plump luscious German nudes. Fair, Aryan, big-hipped bearers of the master race, with which, it was said, the German papers were now spattered under cover of Art, medicine, physical culture, as the Nazis tried to boost war morale with pornography. His mother brought *Picture Post* back with the shopping every Friday. But that Friday he had studied it alone after the others had finished with it, and, as he did so, something had happened to him he would never forget. His body, his whole being, had been suddenly invaded by wave after wave of devastating *sweetness* so overpowering he had nearly swooned and fell back shuddering on the bed uttering a little cry, bewildered as to what had come about. He soon discovered. And how to bring it about. Though never again like that, never in such a dizzying euphoria as on August 28, 1943 when his childhood came to an end with a bang and a whimper.

Voices passed his tent occasionally as men made their way to bed from the canteen, some of them singing. He hoped none of them would blunder into his tent by mistake, like the Glasgow ex-sailor with the huge scar on his scalp. He had insisted on parting his hair to let Joe see and on explaining how he had got it in a thick 'Glesga' patois: it was a souvenir from the Argentine riot police called to Rosie's Place in Buenos Aires when the girls had tried out a little sideline of their own in getting sailors all worked up and then saying, 'You pay more dollar, Johnny boy.' Joe had thought he knew which tent was the Glasgow man's and had very kindly helped him on to the bed but had been awakened later by an awful angry din that told him he had been wrong. He had pulled the blankets over his head and prayed. There were several thick blankets, for it can be cold at nights in the middle of Australia.

'Oh God,' he had prayed, 'what the hell am I doing here?'

What was he doing there? In the middle of bloody Ostralie. In the great red heart of Australia. Perhaps it was something to do with Dandenong; he was not sure what. That time in Belfast when he had suddenly thought: I'll go to Australia. It might just as well have been Canada or New Zealand or South Africa. He could have tossed for it. Maybe Dandenong was his way of tossing for it. It had been in a book of Australian poems by Banjo Patterson he had found in a second-hand bookshop in Smithfield. The man who wrote 'Waltzing Matilda' and the poem about Dandenong. And now they told him it was just a suburb of Melbourne. He had not kept the poems of Banjo Patterson. The event in his life to which they may or may not have given rise was not of the same importance as that for which he kept the *Picture Post* as a souvenir. Now he remembered only three lines. They came to him through the sour taste of his first hangover.

Oft through the mist of my dreams, along
Rides Bannerman of the Dandenong
With a blood-red rose on his breast.

Suez 1956

When Nasser nationalised the Suez Canal in the long hot summer of 1956, girls at parties in the bed-sitting rooms of Earls Court said excitedly that there was going to be another war. The Yanks would come over, they said, and lots of lovely officers would be about. However, other bed-sit girls took a different view and handed out leaflets at street meetings and protest rallies denouncing imperialism and the Eden government. A well-spoken girl from the house where I had a first-floor single sold the *Daily Worker* at the Tube station, calling out things like, 'Learn the truth about . . . the only paper of the workers,' to the dismay of gentlemen from the city in bowler hats, one of whom I saw reproach her sorrowfully in the manner of Gladstone trying to rescue a fallen woman. An elderly gentleman with a room on our second floor was quite shocked. He half-whispered to Danny Prunty and me that Mrs Pusey the old housekeeper had told him that the girl's father was a General and her brother was at Eton. He was something in the administration of the Church of England and had all the old middle-class courtesies, such as addressing you by your surname in order to avoid the rudeness of presumptuous familiarity.

'Who would have believed it, Prunty?' he said mournfully to Danny, who was a back-street Belfast Catholic, 'a girl from a good family, eh, Prunty?'

When the Church of England man came upon a group of us loudly debating the Suez crisis on the landing, and ventured the remark that perhaps Mr Eden was waving the big stick too soon, he was brutally rebuffed.

'He's an imperialist,' they said scornfully.

Ancient and mildewed heads and other big game trophies looked down at us from the walls of the landing and hallway and there was everywhere a musty smell of age and decay. It was probably one of the few bed-sit houses in Kensington still lived in by a member of the family for whom it had once been home, though I did not discover that for some time. One night I heard voices outside my door and when I opened it I was startled by the sight of a tall old lady in a moulting but bright-brown fur coat who called past me into my room, 'Alice, Alice, do come down, there is news from India,' while old Mrs Pusey behind her shook her head at me to pay no attention before gently leading her away. Just after the start of the Suez affair I saw two men in black suits conferring softly in the hall and when I went to pay the rent Mrs Pusey said that Miss Lovibond was dead. I gathered that she had been the old lady in the fur coat. She was to be interred in the family vault in Brompton Cemetery.

'So convenient you know,' said Mrs Pusey with firm cheerfulness.

You could see the railings and some of the taller monuments of Brompton Cemetery from the corner of the street. I once wandered in and strolled along the avenues of the tombs of London's illustrious dead: Admirals, Judges, Inventors, Colonial Administrators. On several there were additional tributes in strange swirling eastern scripts from the grateful subject peoples. There was one in Chinese which made me suddenly remember where I had once before encountered the name Lovibond. It was in St Mary Abbot's Hospital and there had been a little old man in the bed opposite mine called Mr Lovibond, very well spoken but hard up. He had been *most awfully obliged to me* for giving him some cigarettes and, when he saw that I was reading Stevenson's *Travels With a Donkey*, told me that he had done that sort of thing himself, don't you know. In China. He said he had walked across China with a donkey. Had had to shoot the beggar in Chang Ming, he said with the same firm cheerfulness with which Mrs Pusey had described Brompton Cemetery as convenient. Was he, I wondered, what they used to call, in the days of Empire, an old *China hand*? I tried to remember where else I had seen the name Lovibond, perhaps on jars or bottles in the kitchens of my childhood: coffee, ginger, rice, tea? Strolling through the cemetery, I came across a vault, though not the Lovibonds', with a clipper ship carved in stone above the portals. It was like a little house, having a strangely snug-looking glass-panelled front door. At first there seemed to be a cosy little room, in the middle of which was a table and a chair, except that on the shelves lining the walls were coffins. On the table was a jam pot containing freshly withered flowers.

When Mrs Pusey referred to wills going to probate and family having to be traced I was tempted to ask about the old China hand in St Mary Abbot's Hospital but it was none of my business. The house would be sold. We would all have to go.

'Won't we,' she shouted down cheerfully to her two little pug dogs, goggle-eyed and snuffling cantankerously in case they were left out of the conversation, 'we'll all have to go, won't we.'

Men with briefcases were shown round our rooms from time to time, making furtive notes. One of them worried over the identification of item: *head with curved horns*. The fact that we all lived in the imminence of notice to quit gave an extra flavour of change to that Suez summer when Nasser's dark face smiled down upon us from the hoardings, gone jowly with middle age but still floridly handsome with the little lady-killer moustache.

The communist girls on the third floor gave us leaflets explaining that Suez was part of the class struggle everywhere. Everything, it appeared, was part of the class struggle, even Northern Ireland. They gave Danny leaflets on the Irish problem and he learnt to his surprise that Finton Lalor had been a kind of early communist before Marx. Danny had thought that Finton Lalor was the name of a band. The Finton Lalor Hibernian Pipe Band. Danny had only just arrived in

London from Belfast to work in the hotel trade and was still apt to be overawed by girls of the middle and upper classes, having not yet had it proved to him that their anatomy was identical to that of the cockney girls he picked up as easy as wink in Hammersmith Palais and whose voices spoke his name plaintively on the telephone in the hall. Tell him Doreen. Tell him Barbara. He combined Irish good looks with a puritan resentment against women for being desirable – a combination which women found irresistible.

I showed Danny around the famous sights of London and we were lucky enough to view Downing Street on a day when there was a flurry of comings and goings over Suez. The police kept us well back but we witnessed the swerving arrival of black limousines and the slamming of their doors. Someone was hurried into Number Ten amid a posse of tough-looking men who glanced all around them as they moved. The man in the centre was grey-faced, vaguely familiar from his picture in the news.

'Hey, that's Foster Dulles, the American State Secretary,' I said to Danny and added half ironically that we were being brushed by the wing of history. He liked the phrase and got me to repeat it. He was rapidly shedding his broad Belfast accent, though not by Anglifying into that awful Ulster cockney which grates on the ear in both Ulster and England. More subtly, he exploited the resemblances in the Ulster accent to North American, and old Mrs Pusey had delighted him by enquiring if he was a Canadian. He addressed his girls on the hallway phone as *doll*. 'OK, see you around, doll,' he would say, as he brought the latest affair to an end. 'Brushed by the wing of history, doll,' I heard him tell another in just the right tone of raillery to convey an impression of knowledgeability and sophistication. Perhaps she was the pretty little blonde I found in the third-floor kitchen one morning doing his washing and worrying aloud over what she'd tell her mother for being out all night. She wanted me to persuade Danny to go home with her. If only he'd go home with her, she said wistfully, convinced that if her mum met him she would understand.

Soon he no longer needed my tutelage and he knew more about London or 'the town' or 'up West', as he called it, than I did. Instead of Hammersmith Palais girls – or scrubbers, as he called them – it was chambermaids and waitresses from the big hotels. At bed-sit parties he was in great demand for being able to supply delicacies such as smoked salmon, salami and women. He reported seeing many of the famous and the infamous in the hotels he seemed to move around in: the Savoy, Claridge's, Brown's. Sightings of the statesmen who were in the news about the Suez crisis no longer gave him the slightest thrill of being *brushed by the wing of history*. It seemed that men like Nehru, Menzies, Foster Dulles were two a penny in the hotel trade.

The girls on the hallway phone who asked you to tell him Doreen, tell him Barbara now called him not Danny but *Mark*. He thought Mark had more *class*. He sometimes pulled faces at me behind people's backs to get me not to call him Danny. He took a great fancy to reading poetry from some of my books, especially that from the plain rhyming verse department of English literature of which his Irish Catholic education must have starved him. He learnt Coleridge's 'Rime of the Ancient Mariner' off by heart, and Fitzgerald's 'Omar Khayyám'. He was particularly fond of reciting such verses imbued with the sad-sweet hedonism of youth, celebrating the joys of life shadowed by its brevity.

> Dreaming when Dawn's Left Hand was in the Sky
> I heard a Voice within the Tavern cry,
> 'Awake, my Little ones and fill the Cup
> Before Life's Liquor in its Cup be dry.'

He was apt to call on me with smoked salmon and gin after he had been to confession though he would pretend he had been to the public library. The combination of confession and gin made him very candid and poetical. He recited poetry to me and spoke openly about changing his name. It seemed that he would have preferred to be Ralph or Christopher. There was some objection to Ralph I did not quite understand; perhaps it was that Catholics have to have a saint's name and he was not sure about a St Ralph whose bona fides might not, being English, be in favour with the Irish hierarchy. Christopher, on the other hand, would be made common by people shortening it to Chris. I had to agree it was a crying shame what shortening could do to some very classy names. Stephen. Steve. Joseph. Joe. Daniel. Danny. He was quite indignant on the subject and attributed it to the darker side of human nature, with its urge to drag down, deface, defile. I recalled a boy named Alfred who was actually called Alfred, but it must have needed great strength of character. Whereas there was nothing the bums could do about Mark. He had clearly given the matter some thought, and I said that after all if his famous namesakes could do it, why not him? 'What famous namesakes?' he asked, and I said, 'Why, the Brontës, of course.' Emily. Charlotte. *Wuthering Heights* and all that. He had liked the Laurence Olivier film so much that he got the book out of the library and went about being very Heathcliff till it wore off. Emily Brontë.

'Brontë,' I told him, 'is fancy for Prunty.'

'Ah you're codding me,' he said.

I maintained that it was true and what was more I thought they came from his part of the world, but he said I was taking the piss out of him. Lapsing into broad Belfast, the old Danny once more, he said that I was a right oul' cod so I was, though he was intrigued when I said I would look it up in the reference library next time I was there to prove it to him.

When I got home the next evening he was waiting to take me to the reference library. To speed things up he cooked me an omelette. I had never seen one flipped before and it was most impressive. I could visualise him one day performing at table, vanishing in a sheet of flame after they toss in the brandy the way they do, to the ohs and ahs of the ladies, reappearing immaculate and urbane, not a hair singed. Perhaps his own restaurant. Prunty's. Around St James's.

He had never used reference books before, yet he found it while I was still searching. He was very bright. I was looking in the wrong places, in the literary reference books, all about the *works* of. He wandered off round the shelves and came back with a biographical dictionary. He pointed at the entry. BRONTË, Charlotte . . . BRONTË, Emily . . . BRONTË, Patrick, father of . . . Yes! There it was! Clergyman, né *Prunty* . . . humble Irish origins . . . Ballynahinch, County Down!

'The oul' father,' I said in a passable Belfast accent, 'the oul' father made it up for a bit of a cod.'

But Danny, or Mark, as I now had to call him, knew differently. Not for a bit of a cod but for a bit of *class*. And how! One of the most romantic names in literature. Done with just a touch to the spelling. That *ë* with the two dots, hinting at origins exotic and mysterious. Yet made authentic by the true mystery of great art.

'You've been a Brontë all along,' I said, 'without knowing.'

A few days later I noticed a letter addressed to M. Brontë on the hall table. The handwriting seemed suspiciously like his own. Similar letters continued to arrive several times as he savoured the *class* of having been a Brontë all along. He became very familiar with the third-floor communist girls, especially Jennifer, the *Daily Worker* one with the brother at Eton, who was also the prettiest. The girls gave a party at which Jennifer showed him off so much that some of the faithful at first were confused into thinking that he was a new convert. The party was to celebrate some high day in the communist calendar: the October Revolution, the Paris Commune or the Tolpuddle Martyrs, but when I tried to speak to Jennifer about it her attention wandered to where Mark was and once when he sat down near her with his collar ruffled she smoothed it back for him with movements in which the pleasure of touching him were so manifest as to be shameless and, I suspect, would have been so whether he was a Prunty or a Brontë.

'Hasn't Mark got the same lilt as Harry at Cambridge?' a woman called to her husband, who asked her if she was sure, dear, and wasn't Harry from the south, but the woman insisted and appealed to the others to hear Mark's lilt just like Harry's. They spoke with grave concern about what it was like to come from a fascist state like Northern Ireland, and when he looked puzzled they sympathised with him over the special powers of the Northern Ireland police. The secret arrest, they condoled. The midnight knock, they sighed understandingly. They wondered solemnly how long it would be before Northern Ireland fascism spread back to Britain. A nation that oppresses others cannot itself be free, they told each other, obviously quoting somebody. When Mark allowed them to infer quite wrongly that he might be an atheist, though from the Catholic side, they thought this very Irish, very *sweet*, to be a Catholic atheist not a Protestant one, and wasn't he just like Harry at Cambridge, and wasn't it *sweet* the way he said *fillum* for film? When the other women made a fuss of him Jennifer looked unhappy and when I tried to make a joke about the tell-him-Doreen-tell-him-Barbara messages on the hallway phone she made sure it died out feebly by staring at me coldly.

I wondered what he made of the comrades, bearing in mind that the Irish hierarchy held communism in such horror and I chaffed him about it a few days later. But he misunderstood and thought that I disapproved. He chided me for not 'getting around' more and 'taking in' things. 'A young guy should *take in* these things,' he said, meaning in the educational sense, as helping to make a young guy well-informed, interesting, one who had been 'around'.

'Never refuse an experience,' he advised me with a smile not yet as ironic and urbane as it later became when it was accompanied by the raising of *one* eyebrow which I knew for a fact he practised at the mirror for I had caught him at it. He said I shouldn't have created a disturbance at that leftie party, singing like that, a right carry on, he could take me nowhere with a drop of drink in me, what did I want to go singing hymns for?

But he had misunderstood. My hymn singing had been a witty and perceptive comment. Surely he saw that? There had been a great deal of talk, for our benefit, about how naive they had all been before they became 'class conscious'; shaking their heads in wry amusement over how gullible they had been before they learnt about the *class struggle*, how they swallowed their schoolbook history without a thought, how they believed what they read in the 'bourgeois press', how *petit bourgeois* they had been *before*. The word *before* kept recurring. They used to think this before. They used to believe that before. It had reminded me of something, this fond harping on some great watershed experience dividing a life into *before* and *after*. Suddenly I got it. Sinners. Jesus saves. Though your sins be scarlet. Those 'born again' sects where the followers are 'saved'. The testimony giving of those who had dwelt in darkness but have seen a 'great light'. Those to whom truth has been revealed and are set apart because of it, the *elect*. I remember singing the Gospel Hymn at what I felt sure was a very apt moment when one of the third-floor girls described how a pamphlet on Marxism and Women's Fashions had changed her life:

What a friend we have in Jesus
All our sins and griefs to bear –

'You were pissed,' Mark told me, 'that doll thinks you're a bible nutter. It was a right oul' cod so it was.'

I was a little put out by this but we made it up with the help of gin and smoked salmon. I must say that I was becoming very discerning about smoked salmon, its oiliness, texture and colour and could now tell the classy stuff at a glance – to think that I had once regarded the blotting paper in the delicatessen as good! But when I playfully slapped him on the back he let out a cry of pain. He showed me why. There were these marks on his back. Where long-nailed fingers had gripped him arched like claws.

'Bloody women,' he said scornfully, almost angrily, as if the Ulster puritan in him was disgusted at them *all* being like that, at there being none with virtue among them. What, even Jennifer? I wondered. Did ex-public school girls from the shires with a brother at Eton also scratch him in their passion? When she sold the *Daily Worker* at the Tube station or handed out leaflets at street meetings she looked as prim and high-minded as Salvation Army girls selling their *War Cry* or shaking their tambourines. I made a little witticism which I thought quite good, putting on the Church of

England man's manner of addressing him as Prunty.

'It helps in these cases, Prunty,' I said, 'to think of others worse off than ourselves.'

We laughed so much we nearly spilt the gin and he had to keep his back turned from me in case I thoughtlessly rubbed it in about what a cross he had to bear. He said that I was a right oul' cod and should go on the stage.

I asked him if he was not worried about her father the General horsewhipping him. 'Like he did that bounder at his club for insulting the regiment,' I said. I made up another brother who was a Cambridge rowing blue. Was he not alarmed in case a crew of Cambridge rowing hearties wrecked his room? A fellow's sister, dash it, and a bounder! He did laugh a little at this but he also checked with Jennifer that there was no truth in it. Her father the General had cancer and while she had another brother besides the one at Eton, he, it seemed, was still *wetting the bed* at a school of which Danny – sorry, Mark – mistook the type for the name. I explained what a *prep* school was but he preferred Jennifer's description. 'Where they boasted how much their people had stolen from the workers.'

'Did she say that?' I said doubtfully, till light dawned. 'She just meant *rich*,' I said, 'Karl Marx. All wealth is created by work. That sort of thing. *Stolen from the workers*.'

'That's what that doll said,' he confirmed, with an ironical smile to show that he kept an open mind.

He reported another Marxist pronouncement by *that doll* after the gas meter affair. The gas meter in the third-floor kitchen was rifled. Mrs Pusey had wanted to call the police. I had heard a clatter of feet on the stairs and caught a glimpse from behind of a youth whom we all suspected to have been one of the Church of England man's *boys*. He often had visits from boys. One evening his door had been ajar as I passed, and I saw two leering young louts tormenting him by throwing something he valued from one to another as he vainly tried to rescue it, but he firmly shut the door to stop me witnessing any more of his humiliation. Over the gas meter business he made me concede that I had merely *presumed* it was one of his young friends. The communist girls whose room was nearest to the meter would not deign to interest themselves in something so squalidly *petit bourgeois*. Jennifer told Mark that they refused on principle to assist the *class of landlord exploiters*.

At first I wondered when she said these things to him, what with his odd hotel hours and her busy *Daily Worker* selling, her door-to-door leafleting and fund raising for the party by means of jumble sales at which, so far as I could see, the comrades sold each other their old clothes or bought them back again. Perhaps it was pillow talk at night. I thought guiltily of the toilet right next to his back single which was the cheapest in the house, and how carelessly we flushed it in the wee small hours.

Then came the uprising against the communists in Hungary and the news was filled with Budapest as well as Suez. The lights went up in the Kensington Odeon to reveal boy scouts with collecting boxes for the Hungarian freedom fighters; they were stationed in all the aisles, making escape impossible. Earnest debates went on in the third-floor double over the party line. You could hear them at it as you passed by. Sometimes when they had visitors it continued on the landing. One evening Mark and I went into the kitchen to find Jennifer there with a bundle of *Daily Worker*s and a young man carrying one of those portable speaking platforms they used for street meetings. They were indignant about the hostility they were encountering because of Hungary and put it down to the whipping up of anti-soviet hysteria by the jackals of Fleet Street, the hyenas of the bourgeois press.

'Counter-revolution you say, eh doll,' said Mark, cocking an ironic eyebrow, very urbane and cool. It seemed to have a more silencing effect than the street heckling.

The tenants gradually began to move out, the older people first, anxious not to leave it late: it is only the young who find homelessness an adventure. We helped the Church of England man carry down his bits and pieces to the taxi and he shook hands with us in the hallway.

'How nice to have known you, Prunty,' he said courteously.

'Ships that pass in the night,' said Mark, 'and hail each other in passing.'

There was something in the way he said it that was new: a clarity of diction, every word distinct, quite different from the old warm Belfast slurry. I suspected he was practising elocution. I got it out of him on his next confession evening over the gin and goodies. Yes, he was taking in a session or two at these studios in Hanover Street that you hired by the hour. Musicians. Singers. Oh yes, and comedians. *I say, I say, I say, who was that lady I saw you with last night? That was no lady, that was my wife.* He said I should take in a looksee, to hear them at it. *La Donna e mobile.* It was a right old cod, he said, and I noticed he said *old* cod not oul' cod. *Unaccustomed as I am to public speaking.* He said that a guy had to have a bit of class to get anywhere in this *man*'s town.

This confession evening was to be our last. He too was moving out to what he called a new 'pad'. Where, I surmised, he would be Mark Brontë right from what he called square one. It was just after the big rally in Trafalgar Square to protest against the British and French invasion of Egypt. He went with me to 'take it in'. He had recently taken in a symphony concert, a club for queers where they all wore rouge and lipstick, and a Chelsea party where they smoked reefers and knew everybody in television. We heard the great Aneurin Bevan denounce Anthony Eden in his Welsh lilt, mocking the Suez affair as the last twitching of the lion's tail, an old motheaten joke lion. 'Was Eden', he scoffed, 'the front end or the arse end?' All around us were banners and placards. I drew Mark's attention to one held high by the Kilburn Irish: *British Out of Ireland* but he was more interested in the efforts of a small counter-demonstration swathed in union jacks and singing 'Land of Hope and Glory' protected by a cordon of police; from time to time we heard faintly their speaker with a loudhailer saying in an indignant cockney accent something about putting the *Great* back into Britain again. It was all very exhilarating.

The house by then was half empty and I explored the vacant rooms. In the basement I found a small room that had never been let. It was nearest the private park at the back, to which there was an iron gate, rusted and locked. The room was full of ancient deck-chairs, crumbling parasols, a set of croquet hoops and mallets, and a huge archery target with the stuffing coming out, which, on a whim, I looked behind and found an old album of family photographs. I tried to guess which of the little girls or young women in the group pictures could be the old woman in the brown fur coat who had called into my room, 'Alice, Alice do come down, there is news from India.' The young women peered out from under cloche hats in the pictures that were most recent. One snapshot took my fancy: a man in uniform and gaiters bestriding a donkey in a humorous pose, sticking his legs out exaggeratedly in a way that let you know he was used to very different mounts. The hunt. Cavalry. Perhaps polo. I wondered about the old China hand in St Mary Abbot's Hospital.

'Here,' I said to Danny, Mark, Prunty, Brontë, after we had drunk various toasts to this and that: Auld Lang Syne, mud in your eye, next year in Jerusalem, and of course to Patrick Prunty, the founding Brontë father, the 'oul fella himself, 'here, let's have a verse or two of that Boat Song, is it Eton or Harrow? For a bit of a cod.'

I did not expect it to catch on with us as well as it did. But there are certain songs, and indeed hymns, which are very rousing after a glass or two – as anyone will agree who has heard drunken soldiers singing 'The Old Rugged Cross' with heartfelt emotion. We started the song somewhat falteringly and I expected it to peter out on the first verse but instead we were belting it out full throat, squatting on the floor in line and making rowing movements. There were thumps on the ceiling and a rapping at the door.

'One more time,' shouted Danny, 'one more time.'

> Jolly boating weather,
> And a hay-harvest breeze;
> Blade on the feather,

Shade off the trees,
Swing, swing together
With your bodies between your knees.

Jennifer was at the door when I managed to get it open. She gave me a ferocious what-have-you-been-doing-to-him glare of the kind that only doting mothers or lovers are capable of, to which I responded with a little witticism that I thought rather good. I put on a sergeant-major's parade ground bullying manner.

'Git yore nails cut,' I barked at her and then we fell down laughing.

'Ah, he's a right oul' cod so he is,' I heard him say as she helped him to his room.

I was the last tenant to leave. I studied the Rooms Vacant columns in the newsagents' windows. No Irish. No linen. No coloured. Suit business lady out all day. Share K & B. One room I went to look at was already taken and the man was sympathetic to the point of indignation that he had to turn me away. It was all because of *them*, he said, that nice young men like me had a job to get rooms. The chinks and the yellow-bellies, he said, so enraged on my behalf as to be guilty of a tautology. He stood watching me walk away. I knew that he longed to put the *Great* back into Britain again.

But I got fixed up. The evening before I left I answered the door bell. The big-game heads had all gone, leaving bright patches on the bare grey walls. They had been thrown into a scrap lorry along with the old iron. It was Jennifer at the door. Could she have a talk with me? She looked very different in the light of my room. I had never seen her smartly dressed before. Good suit. High-heeled shoes. Nice hat. Gloves. She couldn't have been on her *Daily Worker* pitch dressed like that. I made some feeble joke to that effect. No, she said, she had been to church. I thought she meant some wedding or other among her rich connections, the kind where the women are all rigged out by Bond Street and the men are in tails and toppers.

'It was for Mark,' she said.

I tried to imagine possible errands to the Church undertaken on his behalf by such an intermediary but they were all ridiculous. And where did I come into it?

I was to let him know . . . that she had meant it . . . she really had. She opened her Bond Street handbag and took out a small black book. I was to let him know that she really had taken the first step. The last time she had showed me a book it had been Engels' *The Condition of the Working Class in England.* This was quite different. It was for the instruction of those wishing to be received into the Roman Catholic Church. I was to tell him when I saw him. I had no other purpose. She talked of him for a long time. It seemed to be a relief to her to talk about him. She was hardly aware of my presence. I had difficulty in getting her to go.

I thought sadly of tell-him-Doreen-tell-him-Barbara and – perhaps inaccurately – of Lenin's famous pamphlet 'Who Whom?'

I would miss our little gin and smoked salmon confession evenings, sing-songs, recitations. He had gone off with my 'Omar Khayyám'. Perhaps he recited it in the Hanover Street studios to help along being a Brontë of Wuthering Heights.

> The Grape that can with Logic absolute
> The Two and Seventy jarring Sects confute:
> The subtle Alchemist that in a Trice
> Life's leaden Metal into gold transmute.

The Studios

It had been a dispiriting day for John Quinn. For one thing, when they had sent him to Personnel for a medical the doctor had immediately evinced a marked antipathy for the Irish. When John replied, in answer to a question put without looking at him, that yes, he had been back to Northern Ireland in the past year, the doctor had remarked with a knowing smile to the bustling nurse and the row of impassive waiting men: 'There you are. Probably pay less tax if they come and go. Used to dodge National Service that way.'

'It was my father's funeral,' John exclaimed, but the small seedy doctor dressed in a frayed club blazer did not bother to look up at him.

Then, when with difficulty he got off a little early to eat a pork pie in Lyon's before rushing to the Maida Vale basement flat of Mr Malone Fitzhoward for his singing lesson, he was made to wait a while in the shabby hall before the elderly singing teacher appeared, a warm yeasty smell of bread and tea on his breath, still masticating faintly. John had first met Mr Fitzhoward at a musical event in the Ulster Hall in Belfast where John had sung a small solo part. Mr Fitzhoward had asked him gravely if he had ever thought of having his voice trained professionally and had ceremoniously presented him with his card in case he should ever come to London.

Mr Fitzhoward arranged John in a singing posture at a brass stand with his chin down and hands folded over the groin, shaking him here and there to loosen him. As he made these preparations Mr Fitzhoward spoke indignantly of the jealousy in the musical world that was preventing him receiving the recognition he deserved. It was absolutely disgraceful, he complained, the lengths to which people would go to keep the Fitzhoward Method from gaining wider acceptance. Little black books were stacked high on the baby grand piano. Bright red lettering on them said, 'The Fitzhoward Method'. One letter seemed slightly askew. John had bought a copy after his first lesson and had been disappointed to find that it was full of case histories and testimonials from grateful singers in Melbourne and Sydney and contained little actual description of the Method. When John had timidly mentioned this Mr Malone Fitzhoward had cried 'Hah' in a congratulatory tone, with a little shrewd smile as if to say how clever of John to have spotted that.

'Wouldn't they like to know,' he had exclaimed fervently and had darted at John a pleased look to indicate that he could see that John and he were certainly going to hit it off, 'oh wouldn't they just.'

'Would you believe,' he now said as John placed a school notebook on the lectern, 'that *Voice and Instrument* has returned my card. Some nonsense about the letters after my name. The lengths to which professional jealousy will go would be a revelation to you dear boy.'

'MEE MAI MOH,' sang John in a small sweet tenor, 'MAH MOO MAI.'

Mr Fitzhoward pushed his glasses up on his forehead and listened intently with his eyes closed and his mouth open, joining in occasionally in a fruity baritone.

When he began to prepare new exercises, which was a sign that the lesson was over, John would have liked to remind him that they had started late. Mr Fitzhoward hummed and mouthed sounds like RAH-OH, DAH-OH, LAH-OH, studying John through narrowed eyes as if tailoring the sounds to fit him. Then he scribbled them in a large imposing hand across the pages of the notebook with the tone they were to be sung to.

Was John's local public library, he enquired, making difficulties about ordering *The Fitzhoward Method* for its shelves? John looked unhappily at the clock as he handed over his fee and admitted that he had not yet asked them.

'Oh, do, dear boy, do,' urged Mr Fitzhoward gravely, 'these people should be exposed.'

Barrow men were crying strawberries when he came up out of the Tube at Paddington into the warm spring sun. He carried a little box to his bed-sitting room nearby and stood eating them pensively at the window, sighing occasionally, setting against his feeling of discouragement the luxury of the rich red juicy fruit. He often consoled himself with little solitary snacks of some delicacy or other: smoked salmon, a peach, fruit out of season.

His attic room had a view of roofs shimmering in the spring sunshine. The thought of all that life hidden from view, with its secret pleasures, impenetrable and aloof, evoked in him a confusion of homesickness and sensual longings. He suddenly recalled, without any reason, some note in the prim polite murmurs of Belfast girls that might none the less have promised, though perhaps falsely, the assuagement of desire. He was filled with tiredness and languor. He would have liked to sleep and he looked resentfully at the scattering of books on his little table: *Hugo's Italian Made Easy*, *Hugo's Italian Verbs Simplified*, *The Fitzhoward Method* and an old-fashioned tattered Italian dictionary. Copies of magazines to do with opera and the stage were lying about. His eye caught the little text that he had copied on to a card and hung on the wall. It was a sentence from an exercise in the Italian grammar taken from a writer called Machiavelli. *E meglio a fare e pentirse che non fare e pentirse*. It is better to do and be sorry than not to do and be sorry. It had attracted him and he had made a text of it somewhat self-consciously but defiantly and, as he had been when he first arrived, full of optimism. He turned from it to gaze out of the window again.

He gazed across the daunting roofscape and the vast London sky, thinking of Belfast, of its easy smallness, of the glimpses of hillside and mountain that, everywhere in that drab city, redeem the meanness of its dingy streets and soothe the spirit with images of permanence and serenity. *I to the hills will lift mine eyes from whence cometh my strength.* He had never known the meaning of that text hanging in the parlour at home till now in London, flat, vast, inescapable. He thought of the many times in London when he had been assailed by an intense impulse to try to escape.

There was the day he took a Tube to Epping, thinking hopefully of a walk in Epping Forest. But when he got there he did not like to ask where the forest was so he walked briskly in any direction, keeping an eye open for the trees. He had come to a country road, a real country road, no doubt about it; it was winding, and it had fields on either side, some with cows. He told himself he was getting a bit of country air into his lungs. This, he told himself, is a far cry from Paddington. Any minute and the forest was bound to loom. He had walked and walked. Cars passed him and made him stand well in to the side of the road. All the fields were fenced and had stout gates. He tried standing at the gates, looking over them to let the peace of the country descend upon him but nothing happened of that sort. Every time he turned a bend in the road there was more road. The trees in the distance which he thought might be Epping Forest got no nearer. Wearily he had turned. Cut your losses, he had said to himself resignedly. No use being stubborn, he had decided. Live to fight another day, he put it to himself shrewdly.

As he now looked reflectively at the roofs and chimneys of the capital, he thought of the winding empty road, with the strong fences and the iron gates, that he had traversed in vain, searching for the cool forest. He thought also of when he had first come to London. Then too he had had an impulse to see the country. Why not simply walk till he reached it? he had thought. Get up early. Take a packed lunch. Follow the postal numbers. Plot a rough course north. Steer by the postal numbers on the street names. Save asking. How could you ask where the country was? What country? they would ask back. Any country. Fields. Trees. Winding roads. He had walked with a bold step, feeling young and blithe. He had glanced with disdain at the strange names on the buses which flew past him and which he had no need to know the meaning of, exulting in his cleverness at following the postal numbers. But then it had gone wrong. Long streets began leading into long streets with numbers lower than before. N12 seemed to be succeeded by N2. He began to get angry and bitter. He had felt like appealing to the passers-by to bear witness that it was neither right nor just. But, baffled and defeated, he had given up and turned back, relieved and almost thankful to be once more in the centre of the great web in which he sometimes feared that he was caught for ever.

There was a loud quick rapping at the door and the voice of the housekeeper's daughter Moira calling his name. He had been so sunk in reverie that he blinked at her as if he had been roused from sleep.

'Ah holy Janey,' Moira complained half-humorously in a broad Dublin accent, 'are you drunk or not right in the head or something?'

He had learnt that her brusque scoffing manner was partly a defence, which, out of gawkiness, she thought necessary to adopt in a lodging house full of men, but only partly, for there was indeed something in her nature that scorned and distrusted men. She was a girl of eighteen who could be very pretty when she made up her mind to it and decided it was worth the trouble, which was not always the mood she was in. The only aspect of her looks which did not alternate between prettiness and an almost wilful plainness were her eyes, which were always fine even when she seemed to try to spoil them with a sulky frown.

'Phyllis wants to know,' Moira went on, referring to her mother by her first name and rolling her eyes in a disclaiming way, 'will you go with us to the Crown in Kilburn. That one has been deafening me all day with great reports of that pub. There's a piana and a microphone and the people come forward to make eejits of themselves.'

She had let her shoulders slouch a little, as if not in the mood to straighten them against a slight stoop imparted perhaps by too much carrying around of children for her mother. Her mother had married very young and Moira and she were sometimes taken for sisters. The years of helping to rear her brothers and sisters had given her the right to call her mother by her Christian name.

'I have to go out,' John replied, knowing she would point out that he could come on to the pub later.

'A number sixteen bus,' she explained, 'as if you were setting out for the Galtimore Dance Hall, but,' – and her way of saying BUT in the Dublin accent always fascinated him; to imitate it, as he sometimes did softly to himself, he found it helped to think of, though not quite to say, BUSS, 'but, you be getting off two stops before.'

Her eye caught the books on the table.

'Still at the old Italian, eh,' she said with a scornful laugh and rolling her eyes again, giving him up as incorrigible.

One evening in the basement, when he had smiled at something disparaging that Phyllis said about Moira's passion for rock and roll dancing, Moira had turned on him in a fury. 'Would you look at Harry Secombe there. Think if you learn Italian you'll get singing like Harry Secombe. Think you're the grand fella. But you're not. You're just a poor bloody Paddy like the rest of the poor bloody Paddies.' And she had rushed from the room, leaving him to be mollified by Phyllis and Big Patsy Burke the landlord who sent a crony out for some bottles to make a convivial evening of it. They had persuaded John to sing, calling for order to let him be heard in the now crowded room, shushing Moira as she angrily chased shirt-tailed children back to bed. He had sung them a song from a film musical learnt in boyhood and now somewhat despised, thinking it might be to their taste: 'How are things in Glocamara?'. Their appreciative murmurs that there were no songs like the old songs made him feel guilty, especially when their sense of exile and separation seemed powerfully affected by the list of place names in such lines as 'through Killybeg, Kilkenny and Kildare'. So he had sung them a real Irish song, 'Eileen Aroon', which however had not had nearly the same effect.

After the ball was o'er
What made my heart so sore
Oh it was parting from
Eileen Aroon.

It had filled him with regret for the old times when he had sung it at small concerts and musical evenings back home. Mixed with this feeling was a curious excitement, which, as he made his way upstairs with the air of 'Eileen Aroon' still lingering in his head and met Moira near his room – to get away, so she said, from that bloody knees-up down there – manifested itself as desire. The same desire that came over him now as she stood near his rumpled bed and studied him with wide dark eyes as yet unmarred by her sulky frown.

'Away with you,' she said with a short hard laugh.

'But you did the other evening,' he pleaded, putting from his mind the recollection of his clumsiness and her cry of pain.

'A number sixteen bus,' she called over her shoulder, clattering down the stairs, 'Big Patsy is coming too.'

Big Patsy with his pale fat face that no amount of drink could put colour in; his thin slatternly wife always at her mother's; his charming but authoritative ways; all of which coupled with Phyllis's compliant nature and her still-buxom looks made certain things inevitable. But to Moira's dismay Big Patsy had assumed not only the privileges of a husband but also the duties of a father – and Moira had thought that she was done with heavy-handed fathers. She had risen up against a tyrannical father in Dublin and, in what seemed to John an epic feat of will for a young girl, had organised the flight of the family to London. Moira wanted no more fathers! Yet more and more often did Phyllis invoke Big Patsy's name in quarrels with her daughter. 'Patsy said you weren't to wear your hair like that . . . It won't be well for you if I tell Patsy what you spend on clothes.' Moira, suddenly aware perhaps that her only escape lay in early marriage and that the time between drudging for her mother's children and drudging for her own might well be short, had plunged into a hectic round of rock and roll dancing night after night. One evening she had come home late to find both Phyllis and Big Patsy waiting up for her. John had strained to hear the sharp scream of Moira at her mother, 'Did you not get enough in Dublin?', seemingly followed by a blow. Then there came one night a sharp reminder to John that he could not regard himself as a mere spectator of these domestic struggles. He heard Phyllis railing at Moira that it was nearly one o'clock in the morning. 'What an hour to come in. As well for you it was John Quinn you were with or Patsy would have skinned you.'

He could not pretend to be unaware that he was lingering in the presence of forces and strong wills that could shape his life into something other than his dreams. He looked in panic at the copy of the *Stage* lying open with pencil marks he had put round certain advertisements concerning auditions for the chorus of new productions. He knew quite well that he should flee.

He left the house in haste, carrying a rather elegant little attaché-case as if already in flight. From up the area steps came the bawling of a child and Moira's voice harshly chastising it. The sound made him quicken his steps and he jumped on a bus going to Oxford Circus, where he got off and walked down Regent Street to the place of his appointment. He glanced wistfully at the windows of the smart shops. He liked nice things and had very good taste. He stopped at a famous jeweller's and goldsmith's and studied with satisfaction the small gold cufflinks for which he was saving up to console himself for rebuffs and disappointments, like the early strawberries, like the elegant little leather case he was carrying.

He turned into Hanover Street, and entered a large establishment which displayed grand pianos on the ground floor. A bored man in a little pay booth indifferently consulted a booking ledger.

'Quinn. Eight o'clock. An hour. No piano. Just a stand. Number twenty-two. Six shillings.'

From the floor above came a faint medley of sounds muted by the ceiling. As he climbed the stairs the sounds grew clearer. Scales and exercises from a variety of instruments. Voices not only singing but declaiming. From behind the doors of all the studios, muffled but still audible in the corridor, could be heard practising their skills the many aspiring musicians, actors, actresses, public speakers, those doing elocution exercises in order to rid themselves of plebeian accents.

He was a little before time and the door of number twenty-two was not quite shut. He listened impatiently to two North Countrymen telling the same funny story over and over in loud cheerful voices, stopping abruptly now and then to talk in flat tired tones about timing and gesture. 'There was this fella bought his mother-in-law a blowlamp.' The two would pick up again where they had left off, in rich ringing voices full of laughter.

When the two comedians had gone John opened the window to let out the fetid air, singing as he did so. For a little while he did some Fitzhoward exercises. Then he sang a little piece in Italian with a look of concentration and seriousness that did not entirely correspond with the liveliness of the tune. Then he leafed through the papers in his case and his hand strayed to a very worn song sheet on the front of which was the picture of a merry-looking fat man in a dinner jacket. Harry Secombe the famous singer, the one-time working-class lad who could sing in Italian for the delight of millions and the inspiration of singers like John. 'If I Ruled the World,' John sang in his light pleasant tenor voice which, in the small studio, sounded more powerful than it was. He closed his eyes and lifted his face upwards and made pledging gestures with his hands as he sang of the things he would do for love if he ruled the world.

Opposite the window of his studio was a smart restaurant and those diners with window tables sometimes glanced across in amusement. But not especially at John. They had a view into many of the studios and saw, as it were, a composite tableau of artistic ambition that might have been staged merely as a diversion for them as they wined and dined. But this was an aspect of which John, shedding melancholy and foreboding as he sang, was quite oblivious. In any case he felt that his dreams were of a humbler order than those he sensed in the babel of sound briefly escaping through the open windows of the studios into the evening air before being swallowed up in the unceasing hubbub of London. It was not that great city's acclaim that he dreamt of but of another, smaller city, Belfast, and not even all of that. To walk triumphantly through the small streets he had grown up in; to receive the admiration of the people of his childhood who would remain fixed in his mind as at a certain time; to achieve significance in his native place; these things were all that he asked; these were his modest dreams.

As his song reached its climax he felt a moment of pure happiness, *almost* certain that such a modest dream must surely, surely be fulfilled?

The Streets of Laredo

When the light went out Nigel looked hopefully at Ron to shame him into putting a coin in the electricity meter but Ron made no move. Neither did David. But then it was not David's room and as well as that Nigel owed him money already. The three of them made dark figures in the glow of the muttering gas fire. David said brightly how cosy the room was with only the red glow of the fire to see by. Ron said resentfully that *he* had put shillings in the meter three times running and it was somebody else's turn.

For a while nobody spoke. Then the gas fire began popping and sputtering and finally went out. Again Ron made no move. His voice came out of the darkness, repeating in the same resentful tone what he had said about the light meter except this time about the gas meter. Nigel groped his way to somewhere in the room and the others heard the sound of a drawer scraping open. He struck a match and lit a candle which he placed on a saucer on a large table which occupied the centre of the room. The table was littered with books; a typewriter with a sheet of paper in it; mugs with puddles of old tea on which a white film had formed; the remains of a loaf on a plate. The flickering candlelight made their shadows waver on the walls and the objects on the table seemed to David to make a picture.

'Here,' said David, 'what's-his-name could sell that at his exhibitions.'

'Who?' they said. 'Sell what?'

'This,' said David, 'this scene. That photographer fella at that party. Scene of poor struggling writer. Half starving writer in a garret.'

'This isn't a garret,' said Nigel, 'second-floor double, share K & B, no dogs or wogs.'

'It didn't say that,' said Ron angrily.

'That loaf,' said David eagerly, 'is very good. Very, very good. Maybe a bit nearer that big book. That fella would pay you good money for this. Where's Maguire?'

'Drinking,' said Ron sourly.

'At the BBC,' corrected Nigel reproachfully, 'seeing a man about scripts.'

'Well, drinking at the BBC,' said Ron.

'"For we have a woman, the boulevards roared back, for we have a woman,"' said David, obviously quoting something.

'What's that from?' said Nigel.

'This book about Paris,' said David, 'about the poor lonely writer in Paris.'

'Why couldn't he get a woman?' asked Ron interestedly. Ron had no problem of that kind, being greatly fancied by young bed-sit women of a serious turn of mind, the sort who wore Ban the Bomb badges or little High Church crosses or spoke earnestly about the class struggle. Nigel said it was Ron's red curly beard like Jesus's. Made the church girls feel like Brides of Christ when they took Ron to their beds.

'Ron wouldn't understand,' said Nigel with a sigh.

With the fire out the room grew chilly. First Nigel put on his duffel coat. Then the others did too. Then Nigel drew up the hood of his duffel coat and slowly stretched out his hands to warm them at the small yellow flame of the candle. For a moment the gesture was watched in silence. Then they all burst into laughter. They laughed so much that they had to hold on to the table for support.

'Here,' said Ron, 'why don't we do that when Maguire comes in? Soon as we hear his key in the lock.'

'No, no,' said Nigel deprecatingly, 'it wouldn't be right.'

'"I warmed both hands before the fire of life,"' said David

in the same reciting tone with which he had spoken the words about the womanless writer in Paris.

'Well,' said Ron, 'to show Maguire how things are.'

'Symbolism,' said David, 'very good. Like the loaf and the mugs.' Then he finished what he had been quoting, '"it fades and I am ready to depart."'

'I wish Maguire would depart,' said Ron.

'Ron, Ron,' said Nigel deploringly.

'Yes. Well,' said Ron, a little shamed but defiant, 'we can't afford him. It was all right for a while.'

'Just till he gets these scripts done,' protested Nigel.

'You are angels,' said David, 'you know. *Angels.*'

'What?' they said.

'People who back writers,' said David, 'angels.'

'That's the Theatre,' said Nigel impatiently, 'plays have Angels.'

'Nigel', said Ron sullenly, 'has packed in his job.'

'Just to get Maguire's scripts done,' said Nigel, 'we've been through all this before.'

'Well, you got yer yoof, aintcha,' said David.

'What?' they said.

'Yoof,' explained David, 'cockney for *youth*. This man I met in the launderette with an old dog. Dog smelt awful. Wife left him. Very lugubrious. Tried to cheer him up. *There is still the wind on the heath, brother* sort of thing. Said it was all very well for me. "You got yer yoof, aintcha," he said.'

They burst out laughing. Suddenly everything seemed uproariously funny. The room with the hooded shadows; the guttering candle; the sheet of paper in the typewriter; the sordid dregs of old tea. They had to hold on to the table again, it seemed so hilarious.

'You got yer yoof, aintcha,' they told each other between gasps of laughter, 'you got yer yoof, aintcha.'

'There's a communist party,' said Nigel after they had recovered.

'What?' they said.

'No, I mean this evening,' said Nigel.

'The communist party's every evening,' they scoffed.

'No, I mean a party,' said Nigel, 'this rich communist fella. Maguire was supposed to be going when he got back from the BBC.'

'Then it's a party party,' said David eagerly. 'Hey, that's funny. A party party.'

'What's it for?' said Ron.

'Oh,' said Nigel vaguely, 'you know. The October Revolution. The Dictatorship of the Proletariat. Dialectical Materialism. Marx's Theory of Surplus Value. It's near Harrods.'

'Is it a *Party* party,' said David, 'or a *party* Party?'

'You have to bring a bottle,' said Nigel gloomily.

'All right,' said David, 'I'll be mother. A bottle of British sherry.'

A hostile young woman with an upper-class voice first made them wait till a man to whom she called out 'Do *you* know these people?' came and looked at them and, when Nigel mentioned Maguire's name and nudged David to show the bottle, said with a shrug, 'Oh all right.' Then she tried to take the bottle off them but gave up in disgust when they wrestled with her for it.

They seemed a bit out of things at first. It was a very large room that might have been some kind of studio, having a long table littered with pots and brushes, and, stacked with their faces against the wall, what could have been pictures or posters of the kind people carry on demonstrations and marches, or both. They amused themselves at first with their bottle of VP British sherry, playing a game of hiding it when men arrived, then pulling it out again when girls arrived. People in groups all around them were conducting conversations at the tops of their voices. The three told each other 'You got yer yoof, aintcha,' which still seemed very amusing, as did their alternately concealing and putting on display the bottle of VP. No, they were not dismayed.

'Here,' said David, 'why don't we pretend to be wild Irishmen? You know. Go around saying "Ah Jaysus" to people in a well, *slightly the worse for drink* manner.'

Ron was dubious but Nigel thought the idea funny and

went off to try it on someone he knew in a group arguing about the *bias* of the hanging committee at the Royal Academy Summer Exhibition. He returned saying it was even funnier if you walked a bit unsteadily and rolled your eyes.

David got a chance to try it himself when music was started up at the end of the room and he danced with a pretty nurse from St Mary Abbot's Hospital whom he had grabbed rather defiantly, emboldened by the VP.

'Why do you keep saying "Oh Jesus"?' she asked him none too warmly.

'I don't,' he said, 'it's "Ah Jaysus".'

When he reported this to Nigel and Ron they fell about laughing. Then they were approached by a well-spoken middle-aged man who tried rather wistfully to talk to them about a stuffed fox head on the wall, which, he said, for some reason reminded him of Marshal Tito of Yugoslavia and his standing up to the Russians. A communist *and* a patriot, the man said shyly, did they not agree? When the man went to get himself a drink from among the array of bottles on a trestle table and was seen examining the labels with great interest, Nigel said that he would be admiring David's jersey next. David's jersey was new and of an odd colour that inclined to pink. He had twice been accosted by queers in Earls Court Road since he bought it.

'Yes,' said Ron, 'I think he is one too.'

Sure enough, when the man came back with a glass of something that he sipped rather cautiously, he did admire a jersey – but *Ron's*! David and Nigel thought this funnier than did Ron, and kept bursting out laughing no matter how hard they tried to keep a straight face as the man went on to speak in a wistful way of whether Orwell's *Animal Farm* and *Nineteen Eighty-Four* were as reactionary as the Party people made out. David started to say something about did he mean the party Party people or . . . at which point he and Nigel fell about at the idea of him fancying *Ron*.

'What are you two boys giggling about?' the man said and it sobered them instantly. *Boys. Giggling.* Oh no.

'Oh no we're not,' Nigel and David said, but could not helping adding – to the indignation of Ron – '*we're* not.'

The man looked a bit wry and went away, while Nigel and David mollified Ron by assuring him that they wouldn't start playing that game of telling queers that they'd be all right with Ron . . . only *seemed* hetero . . . that big stud look all a *front*. No, they wouldn't really. Not after what happened last time. In any case they found the wild Irishman idea funnier.

'If only we had the nerve,' said David.

'What?' they said.

'Pretend to mistake that bedroom where the coats are for the toilet,' said David. 'Ah Jaysus.'

Nigel and David were overcome. They tried incoherently to convey to Ron the comedy of a wild Irishman swaying unsteadily as he pissed all over the coats, but Ron thought they had gone too far and stroked his beard primly. They asked him what he had put on that prim look for and he said, 'Well.'

'Well what?' they said.

'All that Sambo stuff,' he said.

'What Sambo stuff?' they said, and Ron muttered about racialism and anti-semitism and that *he* voted Labour. He didn't approve of all that Ikey and Sambo stuff.

'Where?' they said.

'Well, Paddy jokes then,' said Ron, angrily stretching curls in his beard and letting them go. He muttered that Paddy and Mick jokes led to Ikey and Sambo stuff.

'Who's that?' said David, pointing at a newcomer whose arrival seemed to be causing a stir, a very old man with a wrinkled face but dressed exotically in a black wide-brimmed hat and a huge orange bow tie. A crowd of young men had gathered deferentially around him, hanging on his every word, laughing loudly at all his quips and sallies. Ron nudged David at the fact that Nigel was also very impressed though trying to sham indifference.

'The *Lyceum*,' said Nigel in a studiedly offhand way, referring to one of the poetry magazines of which he was an avid reader, 'that's the old bird who puts money into it.'

'They say,' said Nigel even more casually, for he was suspected of writing poetry and not just, as he claimed, of being *interested* in the new wave, 'they say he saved *Orion* from closing last quarter.'

'"Plughole"' said David, 'a new-wave poem. Words such as glug-glug arranged in diminishing circles spiralling into empty centre so that reader has to rotate page at increasing speed.'

'That lot there,' said Ron scornfully, referring to the group of young people around the old Bohemian, 'that shower. All poets. Sucking up to that old creep to get their stuff printed.'

'"And live alone in the bee-loud glade,"' David recited oddly in a high-pitched monotone.

'What?' they said angrily.

'Yeats,' David said, but they said, 'Yes, well?'

'That's how Yeats spoke it,' said David, 'in a thin scream.'

'How do *you* know?' they demanded.

'The radio,' said David. 'Heard this awful recitation. Some awful poetry goon of the new wave,' they supposed. 'No. Yeats himself. Early recording. Dreadful screaming. As bad as that poetry reading we went to in Fulham.'

'What poetry reading?' said Ron suspiciously.

'You didn't go,' Nigel explained placatingly.

'Big row at it,' said David, 'punches were thrown.'

'Why wasn't I at it?' said Ron accusingly. But Nigel had edged them nearer the *Lyceum* publisher and his orbiting disciples.

The old man's wrinkled face was a study of fastidious sensuality and the young people around him were chidingly refusing to believe his protestations that he was no longer able to – as he put it quite candidly – satisfy young women sexually. His diction was beautiful and distinct. Like well-cooked rice. Every grain separate. He particularly hissed the sibilants, as in *satisfy* and *sexually*.

'Oh come, J.D.,' his young entourage reproved him, exchanging looks that he was meant to see and be flattered by. It seemed that he was always referred to and addressed by his initials. 'Oh come, J.D. What about your harem of poetesses?'

J.D. conceded, in exquisitely enunciated words with a sharp hissing sound on the end of poet*ess*, that a young poet*ess* had indeed taken him to her bed that very afternoon, but, and he raised an old spotted fist with the thumb protruding limply between the first two fingers, her many and exotic arts were unavailing.

'*Anno Domini*, dear boys,' he said grandly, 'life's waning fires, dear boys, life's waning fires.'

Ron and David fled precipitately out of range so that they could fall about laughing, though Nigel made little deprecating signals to them to tone it down when they shouted to him about his 'yoof', and then pretended that he had nothing to do with them.

Ron and David started playing a new game. They repeated to each other with exaggerated sibilance the words 'sexually satisfy'. They rolled about laughing and slapped one another on the back.

'Six poetesses,' they sibilated exquisitely, 'sexually satisfied on the summer solstice.'

Then they challenged each other to do it with a lisp. *Thickth poetetheth*. For a time they would not allow that either had done it successfully. You said *thummer tholstice*. You said *thummer tholstith*. Take it slowly. They watched one another's teeth. People gathered to see what they were doing. When Ron bared his teeth and protruded his tongue exaggeratedly to prove he had not cheated on an apparently clear run a girl with a ponytail and a Ban the Bomb badge asked David if Ron was French; was it, she wanted to know, an exercise in English for Foreigners? They explained to her about the old lecher in the orange bow tie. 'You're not a poet*ess*?' they hoped gravely. 'Goodness no!' There was a silver crucifix round her neck. Ron put his arm round her. David withdrew diplomatically and tried his luck again with the St Mary Abbot's nurse, but she was as unamused by the poet*esses* story as by the wild Irishman pose. He found Nigel with the artist fellow they knew vaguely; they were discussing how to get Nigel a session or two posing nude for the life class at the RA. Would try his best. Might have to stand this man a few beers. What about the evening classes game? What, show the family heirlooms to suburban housewive's art classes! Oh I say, dash it! Steady on! A fellow has his pride!

Where was Ron? When David said that this girl was High Church *and* Ban the Bomb *and* at a Party party they agreed that they were unlikely to see Ron again that night, but to their surprise he joined them soon afterwards. What, nothing there tonight? No. Well. He was seeing her tomorrow. Trafalgar Square. Where! The Ban the Bomb demo. Michael Foot was speaking. So it would be *tomorrow* night then! What did they mean! He believed in it, Ron claimed indignantly, he *believed* in it.

'Here,' said Nigel, 'let us betake ourselves elsewhere.'

'"To fields where flies no sharp and sided hail, and a few lilies blow,"' said David.

'There's that folk-song coffee bar in the King's Road,' said Ron.

'Quite,' they said.

The folk-song coffee bar was in a cellar. There were candles in old wine bottles, rush matting on the floor and posters on the walls advertising music hall performances for dates in November 1892, bull fights in Madrid in 1934, and constipation in 1922. There was an authentic early Edison phonograph up on a shelf on which Nigel said he had heard Dame Nellie Melba sing 'Home Sweet Home' on a wax cylinder before they had had to put it up on the shelf to stop people mucking about with it. There was a small stage on which a young man was singing as they came in and they got as near to it as they could with their mugs of espresso.

The young man had a guitar and he sang in the very relaxed way that was all the fashion and was not in the least put out by the murmur of conversation that went on during his singing. The clientele for their part showed how much they appreciated his singing as a background to their earnest discussions by sending up requests for other authentic ballads such as 'Barbara Allen' or by clapping tastefully when he strummed the guitar in a moderately wild Spanish style between the verses of 'Dublin City'.

> As I went up to Dublin city
> About the hour of twelve at night
> Whom should I see but the Spanish Lady
> Combing her hair by candlelight?

'Ask him for that Irish cowboy song,' said Ron, 'that one of Maguire's.'

'Maguire's Irish cowboy song. Right.' said David, half-rising in pretence that that was what he was going to request.

'No. No,' said Nigel, pulling him down. 'It's "The Streets of Laredo". This BBC script. Migration of ballads. Old Irish song. *List to somebody's sad lay.* Crossed the Atlantic at the Famine or the gold rush or something. Became "The Streets of Laredo". So Maguire says.'

'Hey,' said David, 'speak of the Irish. Look! or List!'

There was a commotion at the bottom of the iron staircase. The disturbance arose from a group of men trying to squeeze themselves round a table. They had broad Irish accents of the working class and wore what were obviously their Sunday suits – though not all with ties – which alone would have set them apart from the casual jerseys and jeans around the coffee bar. Nigel and Ron whispered at David to keep his voice down. The men, though not young, looked very formidable and had deep, building-site tans. One of them produced a bottle and liberally laced all their coffees. They surveyed their surroundings amiably and looked at the small stage with interest. Somebody called Patsy was urged loudly to get up and give them a song *so* like a good Christian. One of the coffee bar girls went over to them and said nervously that the premises were not licensed for the consumption of alcoholic drinks and they told her that she was a *lovely* girl, a *lovely girrul*, so she was, and Patsy was going to give them all his pleasure. A small bull-necked man in a blue serge suit with a collarless shirt mounted the stage and coughed to clear his throat. 'Quiet for the singer now! Shush for Patsy! Order on the floor now!'

The coffee bar girls and the official folk-singer conferred at the espresso machine. The mainly young middle-class clientele steeled themselves for what they thought could only be a painfully embarrassing demonstration of the cultural gap between themselves and the working class on the booze. Was it going to be some awful old-fashioned pop song done in the awful old-fashioned pub/seaside outing manner, strident and off-key? 'Mammy'? 'The Sunny Side of the Street'? 'And You Were Temptation?' Would he go down on one knee doing 'Mammy'? How awful.

But it was not like that. Patsy arranged himself in a formal concert-hall posture with the hands folded at the groin. Then, making not the slightest concession to changes in public taste in over half a century, he sang, in a rich fine tenor, a Victorian drawing room ballad: 'I Dreamt That I Dwelt'. His beautiful voice disarmed the audience and won them over and perhaps also something in the song itself, that odd Victorian quality, which, even as its sweetness cloys, still has the power to move.

> I dreamt that I dwelt in marble halls
> With vassals and serfs at my side,
> And of all who assembled within those walls
> That I was the hope and the pride.

'Would your friend know "The Streets of Laredo"?' David asked very respectfully of the largest of the Irishmen, the one who had called for order and who now enthusiastically led the applause when the song ended. David was made to repeat his request several times before it got shouted up correctly to Patsy. He had to think for a moment or two. He was clearly not used to being asked for it and his cronies looked somewhat displeased at David, as if they suspected him of being a troublemaker, but alarm was dispelled when Patsy nodded and the Irishmen broke out into cries of congratulation. 'He does, begod,' they told each other admiringly, and the large man told David sternly that Patsy had music in him that would astonish the world.

At first Patsy sang 'The Streets of Laredo' in the same

manner as before, which was rather inappropriate for a cowboy song, but gradually his posture and his style changed. A keening plaintive note came into his voice, rough and primitive, and he sang the words with heavy emphasis on the rhythm. One of his friends began to keep time with his foot, lifting it off the floor in heavy tramps. The cellar with its flickering candlelight took on the aspect of an Irish cabin filled with music making.

> As I rode out in the streets of Laredo,
> As I rode out in Laredo one day,
> I met a young cowboy all wrapped in white linen,
> All wrapped in white linen and cold as the clay.

In awe they watched, as it were, the song returning home.

> 'I see by your outfit that you are cowboy,'
> These words he did speak as I slowly passed by.
> 'Come sit down beside me and hear my sad story,
> I'm shot in the breast and I know I must die.'

They still had the song in their heads as they walked home through the silent night streets. They were very subdued. Without any fuss Ron stoked both meters with coins and flooded the room with warmth and light.

There was nothing for breakfast. They looked in the cupboards of the chaps from the third-floor double with whom they shared the kitchen but it was full of old milk bottles – a matter of grievance to the milkman who had raised his voice about that and his unpaid bills in the hallway several times. One of the chaps came in on the same errand and shook an empty cornflakes packet from Nigel and Ron's cupboard. 'Perhaps David downstairs?'

'He has no milk,' Ron said, 'somebody swiped it.'

'Tst, tst,' they said deploringly. Then one of the chaps said that there was this pub in Kensington High Street where they put plates of cheese on the bar on Sunday mornings.

'What, free?'

'Yes, free.'

'Well,' they said, 'what are we waiting for?'

So duffel coats were donned, David was knocked up, and off they set.

On the way they conversed eagerly on the topic that was the bridge between them all, which was the fascinating novelty of bed-sitting room life. They spoke of how much they owed in back rent; of cheap foods like black puddings; of the vagaries of landlords; of whether sponging with vinegar would stop a girl getting pregnant; of famous people met at parties; or the fiddling of rapacious gas meters. One of the chaps related how old so and so had had to go to his job in this broker's office wearing white tennis slippers because his room-mate had borrowed his shoes, which on the whole they considered a bit much – a chap's shoes dammit! – but they laughed so much they had to hang on to each other for support. They spoke of these matters not only with hilarity but with a kind of excited awe at things that were part of the great shared adventure of being young in London and away from home. David said something about *yoof* but they told him not to start that again, and he said, no it was *Conrad*'s 'Youth'. '"That which while it is yet expected,"' he prompted them. 'You know. "Is already gone."'

'Yes,' they said vaguely.

'"In a sigh, in a flash,"' said David.

'Where is this cheese pub?' they demanded impatiently.

But they came to it in time and it was quite true about the cheese. There it was, spread out hospitably on the counter. Large plates of cheese cut up into little cubes. People drinking just helped themselves. There was only one snag. Why had they not thought of it before? Who was buying? Nigel? Not him! David? Sorry. The chaps? Skint! They looked at Ron. They fixed their collective gaze upon him with great intensity.

'Oh no,' he said resentfully, fingering his beard, 'oh no. Not me again.'

But, they pointed out, he was the only one with money. How did they know that? he protested, pulling at his whiskers. He could be skint too, they weren't the only ones. But they said not to perjure himself. Everybody knew. What? That he was, well, very careful with money.

'Pawky,' suggested one of the chaps diplomatically. 'Like the Scots,' he explained when they looked puzzled.

'You mean *canny*,' they said.

'Pawky,' David said, 'means sort of drily humorous.'

'*He*'s not drily humorous about money!' Nigel scoffed, 'look at him! Salts away every penny.'

Salts. Drily. They hung out their tongues.

'Ah well,' said Ron, 'that's for France.'

France? Nigel explained with an amused half-apologetic air that Ron saved up all winter so he could lie about all summer in France drinking wine.

'That book is out,' said David to Ron reproachfully, 'about French torture in Algeria.'

'Just *one* round,' they said to Ron, 'to go with the cheese. That's what friendship means.'

Ron went up to the bar while the others settled themselves round a table, calling after Ron their wishes in the way of drinks. A Grand Marnier shandy. A Château Lafite and mild. A Taylor '28 with just the merest squeeze of barman's armpit. 'Oh look,' they said, 'he's got out a purse! Oh Gawd! He's a *purse* type.'

Ron came away from the bar with a plate of cheese and a single half-pint of brown stout which he proceeded to drink with determined unconcern. They ate the cubes of cheese and watched Ron drink. They watched him the way a dog watches people eating, following every movement of the glass with their heads as well as their eyes. The landlord appeared at their table looking very tense.

'I must ask you to leave,' he said tensely, 'please drink up and leave.'

Well! Leaving was one thing. But drinking up! The landlord must mean their pawky colleague.

'Why don't you do what the man says?' they said sadly to Ron.

Outside in the empty Sunday street of shuttered shops they

wondered how many pubs it was now that they were barred from.

'I do wish', said Nigel to the chaps, 'you wouldn't eat our cornflakes.'

'"For noise is not in the market place but in the changing hearts of men,"' said David.

'What's that from?' they said.

'Oh it sounds well but doesn't mean anything,' said David deprecatingly.

'You wrote it yourself,' they accused.

'No, no,' David protested modestly.

'Are you a poet too,' the chaps said reproachfully, 'like Nigel there?'

'No, no,' said David with a smile.

'No, no,' said Nigel, 'Ron puts that about.'

'Now about this food problem,' they said, and pressed their noses against the window of a delicatessen shop with its mouth-watering display of cooked meats and delicious-looking little tubs of made-up dishes. Smoked salmon. Salt beef. Olives. There were huge uncut cheeses and great bunches of uncut salamis.

'What a pity Trevor isn't about anymore,' Nigel said.

Trevor? Oh him. Yes. Oh yes. Used to bring back whole salamis from that hotel he worked in.

'He's in Brixton now,' Ron said grimly, and they said, 'What? Brixton *prison*? Just for a few salamis?' But Ron said that he thought it was for HP. Getting stuff on HP and selling it. Tried to flog *him* an electric guitar and a set of drums.

Somebody said, 'Wasn't Trevor writing a book, didn't he show it to people?'

'I hate people who do that,' Ron said, 'show you their stuff for you to say how good it is.'

'There you are,' they said to David, meaning the lines he had spoken about noise being in the hearts of men, 'there you are. You be careful. You'll lose friends that way.'

'But I don't,' David said. But they said he *might*; any day now; working up to it; on the brink of *showing people a manuscript*.

'Trevor', said Ron, 'watched you while you read it.'

'Oh my God,' they said, aghast, 'they are the worst. No wonder he's in Brixton!'

Ron said that Trevor took him into Routledge's Hotel one night and he saw the cockroaches. What! Cockroaches! Routledge's! But the Shah of Persia stays there!

'Yes,' Ron said, 'Trevor thought he had dropped his pen in the breakfast pantry. Got the night porter to let us look. These big beetle things. Soon as he switched on the light. Trod on one. Heard it crunching.'

'They say,' said one of the chaps gravely, 'that some of the clubs have them,' and Nigel said that ships all have them. Nigel had been an officer cadet on a cruise liner for a time after leaving his school, which was almost, though not quite, a public school.

'The galleys all have them,' Nigel said, 'they fumigate the galleys in port but they always come back.'

'Galleys.' David repeated the nautical word admiringly and asked the chaps if they knew that Nigel was an old salt. 'A real old seadog, one of your genui*wine* don't make them like that anymore, rum bum and baccy jolly tars.'

'What was Trevor's book about?' they asked.

'Life,' said Ron.

'Life!' they scoffed.

'Well that's what Trevor said,' Ron said.

'Was it life or Life?' they asked, and found this so funny they slapped each other's backs and fell against one another.

No, seriously, they told each other, they must eat. What with some serious drinking to do at that party later on. What party? Oh that one. Yes. Must forage. Get a lining on the stomach first.

They parted at the corner of Earls Court Road and went their several ways to which they made laconic reference. Fiona and Prue still good for a bowl of soup. These BBC scripts if Maguire turns up. Hear Michael Foot in Trafalgar Square. And David? Oh you know. Stroll about. Idly saunter through the streets. The Streets of Laredo.

'You watch it,' they called back at him warningly, 'you

watch that *noise not in the market place* business or you'll end up like Trevor.

'"All wrapped in white linen,"' they called with a laugh, '"and cold as the clay."'